All Weekend with the Lights On

D1568252

Also by Mark Wisniewski

Writing and Revising Your Fiction   (The Writer)

Confessions of a Polish Used Car Salesman   (Hi Jinx Press)

The Dialogue on the Other Side of the Door   (Showerhead Press)

ALL WEEKEND WITH THE LIGHTS ON

SHORT STORIES
BY

MARK WISNIEWSKI

Leaping Dog Press

CHANTILLY, VIRGINIA : 2001

Acknowledgments

The author and the publisher wish to express their grateful acknowledgments to the following publications in which these stories first appeared: "Three-Quarters Stitched" in *Black Warrior Review* and the web magazine *Crossconnect*; "Pocket" in *Kansas Quarterly* and the anthology *Anyone Is Possible* (Red Hen Press); "Unknown Rook" in *The Chariton Review*; "3 x 5 Steve" in *Bakunin*; "Undiscovered" in *Art:Mag*; "Pushing Ahead" in *Colorado North Review*; "Night Vision" in *Lime Green Bulldozers*; "Airstrip" in *The Macguffin*; "Trust" in *Angelflesh*; "Birdie" in *The Missouri Review*; "Confession" in *Paris Transcontinental* and *Gulf Coast*.

Cover design by Elizabeth Rendfleisch and Jordan Jones.

ISBN 1-58775-002-3 (paper)
ISBN 1-58775-003-1 (electronic)
Library of Congress Catalog Number: 00-108700

This book has been printed on recycled, acid-free paper, by McNaughton & Gunn, Saline, MI, and has been published in an edition of 1,200 copies, of which the first 100 are signed and numbered by the author.

This is number _____ of 100.

Leaping Dog Press
PO Box 222605
Chantilly, VA 20153-2605
www.leapingdogpress.com

Contents

ALL WEEKEND WITH THE LIGHTS ON

Three-Quarters Stitched

With a diamond ring in my apron chest pocket I'm kneading eggbread dough, and the gushy warmth around my fingers reminds me of whoopee with Junie, and I tell myself, as I knead, that I shouldn't marry for whoopee only. I divide into thirteen loaves and bake and remove, and during cooling Waju, my brother who runs the bakery with me, walks in through the rear door. Waju is twenty years older because Ma had him eight months after she and Pa married, and me ten years before they died and left us the bakery—me a year after they figured her time for children was done. Waju is married to Sophie, who I saw cheating on him while they were engaged and he was cooking for the lines in the Big One. With Pinky of Pinky and Jo-Jo's Bowl, she was cheating, right on the hood of Pinky's Ford, with *she* on top telling *him* to relax, and she might have seen me see her but never said a smidge about it, just gave me a look the next day I'll always remember and still sometimes see when she waits with a sale for the cash register.

See, Sophie helps us at the bakery sometimes. Anyway she's not there when, like I say, Waju walks in through the rear door. Where she is I don't know, and Waju probably don't either, and he looks at me like he's got good news and says, Let's see it.

What, I say.

The diamond.

I stick a finger in my chest pocket and feel nothing, so I stick in two and feel all the way into both corners, then pat all my pockets with both hands, powdering my *dupa* with flour.

So you're still chicken, he says.

No, I'm not, Waju. I bought it and had it in this-here pocket. And it's gone.

With wings it flew out?

No jokes now, I say. I paid four months' profit-share for that thing.

The door to the storefront opens and Sophie walks in. She ignores Waju as usual and grabs an eggbread and sets it in the slicer and flips the switch. What's gone, she says, giving me her look.

Nothing, I say before Waju can answer. I don't want him to tell her what's gone because of course she don't like me and if she knows my intentions she'll fib to Junie bad stories about me so Junie'll say no when I propose. And then, to convince Junie, I'll have to explain that Sophie said this and that because she don't like me because I witnessed her wartime cheating, which means Junie might then mention the cheating to Waju—and I don't want Waju to feel hurt. Hurt he's had enough of. Before he met Sophie, when he played baseball semi-pro, he loved an Irish girl Kate, and Kate was gentle like an angel and loved him as if he were Christ, but he took her night-fishing one November and she caught a pneumonia Dr. Vraszak couldn't cure.

But you said something was gone, Sophie says now. Waju and I look at each other, and she turns off the slicer. Jesus in limbo, she says. Lost a finger. She says this calmly, like she usually talks, and she's always fibbing about health problems—corns, bunions, ringing-in-the-ear, cancers—so I don't look over, just again pat my pockets.

Waju walks toward Sophie quickly, which isn't like him, and stoops in front of the slicer and picks up something pink. No blood on it, but then I see drops falling off the slicer blades faster than rain from the top of a clogged downspout, and Sophie has a look on her face I've never seen—like an infant sleeping, she looks—so I know she ain't fibbing. Waju holds the

4

bloody hand high and says to her, Okay, let's relax. And to me he says, Get a clean washrag.

All used, I say.

Then a dirty one.

No dirty one, Sophie says, fainting against his side. Use an eggbread, she says, and Waju shrugs. So I walk a loaf over and Waju hands me the loose finger-half and holds the bleeding stub steady and brings down the soft side of the loaf so the stub plugs on in through the crust. He takes her good hand and has her with him hold the eggbread steady, then leads her out the rear-door, and I follow.

We get into their Rambler with Sophie sitting between me and he, with me now holding up and steady the eggbread and she resting her head on my shoulder. She fades enough to look gentle, almost like Kate, and Waju misses a stop sign, and the sliced-off piece in my palm cools like a miniature cruller.

We pass St. Josaphat's, where they married, and I realize he's headed *away* from the hospital. To emergency, no? I ask.

To Vraszak, he says. Emergency takes forever.

Vraszak's no surgeon, I say.

He stitches, he says. He stitched my shoulder good that time I tore it up sliding into third.

And he owes us for ham, Sophie mutters. So when he bills, we can call it even.

Relax, Dear, Waju says, and I wonder: Where's that gosh-darned ring? I took it from my pocket before I began kneading? I wonder, and Waju floors the pedal. I wonder too what Junie is doing, and I look at Waju biting his lower lip and Sophie gentle only because she's woozy and think: This is family. And family is what happens to love.

At Vraszak's, Waju explains to the typist what happened and she says to sit, and Sophie says Vraszak owes us for six pounds ham—and we get in. Vraszak is on the other side of the wall vaccinating Virgie Gladowski's screaming little ones, and for a second I think maybe it's good the ring's gone: maybe I should reconsider marrying. See, I don't take screaming well, never have. Waju does, but that's because, when he played the semi-pro baseball, fans for the teams he'd pitch against would scream cuss-words at him in the ninth inning, so, to him, screaming means he's almost to victory. His problem now, though, is silence, because Sophie and he never scream anymore. In fact, they rarely talk. As his brother I know this bothers him—and too that he ignores why it bothers him—and, as we three sit watching the jars of tongue depressors and cotton balls, I understand why he prefers to ignore: his wife just lost half a finger and he's holding her good hand and scratching her back soft-like—and she still won't say boo. I still have the sliced finger-piece half in my hand when Vraszak closes the door and says, How are we?

Minus half a third finger, Waju says.

Let's see, Vraszak says, and Sophie raises the eggbread, which Vraszak removes and tosses there in his wastebasket, and blood runs. Minus it is, he says. You bring the remainder?

I hold out my hand and open.

Clean slice, Vraszak says. Good.

He steps to a table and gets a needle and brown stitch-thread. He has a blind man's time threading the needle. Keep your arm up on an angle like that, he tells Sophie. So I can see what I'm doing. Then he takes the piece from my palm, rinses in alcohol, and goes to work.

While he stitches, he talks. His voice is the only sound in the room except the snips of the scissors and a Gladowski girl crying, and he talks about his last vacation up north to Door County, and how he and his wife took walks there and got to talking about their younger days—and how their talk helped them again fall in love. Sophie, while he talks, is gazing at the ceiling, and Waju is watching the needle, and I'm looking back and forth between them knowing they know that Vraszak knows Waju loved Kate and don't get along with Sophie: Vraszak is not only trying to attach two finger-halves, he's trying to attach two hearts. And because no one's answering him makes me sure he'll fail. He might get that finger to heal itself together, but those hearts, Waju's and Sophie's—forget it.

After he announces stitch sixteen, he quiets to sew only, and I keep thinking Where's the ring? I need to find it because it cost hundreds, and I need to give it to Junie to keep us loving because she herself has been quiet lately, and that bothers me. The ring, I think, should get her talking again. Then I think: What if it don't?

You need me here still? I ask Waju.

No, Vraszak says.

Waju? I ask. Okay if I go?

How will you get back? Sophie asks.

Walk, I say. I want my brother to answer, but all he does is watch the two finger pieces, which are three-quarters stitched but still apart. I tell myself there's nothing I can do, then tell Sophie good luck, squeeze Waju's shoulder and leave them to themselves and Vraszak's stitching.

Outside the office, I run like on fire. I pass St. Josaphat's, where I too will marry—if Junie wants. I realize I left the bakery's rear door unlocked and run faster. And if I don't find that ring, I think, *I* might lose the love of my life. I think about how last I was over eating dinner with Junie and her parents, this guy my age Bruno, the son of Pinky of Pinky and Jo-Jo's Bowl, called and asked her out. I think about how she didn't say yes but stayed on the phone long, and how, while they talked, her ma offered me more meat-loaf, more pierogies, more gravy and more kapusta, and how maybe the reason her ma was extra-nice then was because mothers don't like men who make secret whoopee with their daughters—and she knew more about Bruno and Junie than I do.

I reach the bakery's rear door and run in. For the ring I look on the floor, on and under the trays, in the open flour sack I used, between lard cans, under the silver tables, in the bathroom, around the bloody slicer, but: nothing. The phone rings and it's Junie asking if I want to go bowling later. Sure, I say, and I tell her I'm busy and hang up because maybe the ring is in one of the eggbreads I baked—and I see that they're gone off the cooling rack. I run out to the storefront, where the customer door rings shut and the

Lutz girl is closing the register. I glance at the eggbread shelf and count twelve. Something wrong? the Lutz girl says.

You sell an eggbread? I say.

Yes, she says, and she smiles to show to me her teeth, which are yellow and crooked but sexy.

You're kidding.

Nope, she says. I talk up your product and move it.

The Lutz girl, I know, is sweet on me. She's always grinning those teeth and asking about honey-glazed donuts when she slides cookies in the counter so I can see her rising uniform-dress show her thighs. She's too young for me, the Lutz girl, maybe eighteen or so, and she *is* an employee, and anyway I love Junie and when I love, I love one and that's it.

Shoot, I say.

Why shoot?

Because I need it.

Need what? she says winking.

That eggbread.

A fresh cherry-filled won't do?

No. That eggbread might have something in it I need.

Like what?

It's a secret. Who bought it, anyway?

Pinky, she says.

Bowling lane Pinky?

Yeah. His family's having a big-to-do dinner now. And he told me a secret of his own.

I picture Pinky's son Bruno slicing the eggbread and finding the ring—and using it there to propose to Junie.

Trade? the Lutz girl says.

What you mean?

You tell your secret and I tell Pinky's.

I can't, I say.

Why not?

Mine's personal.

So is his.

I think: She and Pinky know Bruno and Junie are making whoopee. Then I think, No. You're in love and imagining jealous.

Come on, she says. You'll find it interesting, she says, and she licks her teeth in a softer smile that pulls me toward her.

Interesting? I say.

Sure, she says, lifting her uniform skirt to scratch above her garter-snap.

Sex, I think. Everyone wants it—not just those hippies on communes. Okay, I say.

You first, she says.

I want to tell her *You* first, but I know she'll flirt back, and Bruno right then could be slicing. So I tell her, I lost a ring. And it might be in that darned eggbread.

Her eyebrows form the shape of those-there McDonald's arches. What kind of ring?

None of your business, I say. Just tell me your secret so I can go look.

She puts her lips so close to my ear I get gooseflesh, and a customer walks in, Mrs. Stahowiak.

Hurry, I whisper, because the Lutz girl's breath tickles and Mrs. Sta-howiak is looking and I don't want this scene back to Junie.

Pinky's family, the lips whisper, is eating Little Karen's pet rabbit.

Who's Little Karen? I whisper.

Pinky's daughter. You know, Bruno's sister.

Mrs. Stahowiak faces the day-olds, so I enjoy the gooseflesh a little longer. That's a good secret? I say.

Why sure. Because Little Karen don't know. Pinky told her he gave the rabbit to the Human Society because she wasn't feeding it regular. But see, he didn't give to the Human Society. He had it *field*-dressed—by Norm Skoronek.

The gooseflesh is so good I feel how easy a couple can cheat.

And in a low voice the Lutz girl says, Interesting, inna?

They're eating the rabbit right now? I ask.

Yeah. They're making the meal a big to-do so no leftovers raise her suspicions.

A dozen prune-filleds, Mrs. Stahowiak says, and the Lutz girl touches my arm and walks off.

Put them eggbreads in back, I yell at her as I run to the customer door. And don't let nobody touch them.

Then I run to Pinky's house, which everyone knows is his because it's three stories he afforded with all that shoe rental money—and because his wife Jo-Jo painted it pink. I ring and knock and ring, and a little girl answers, and I say hello and she says, I'm Karen, who are you?

I need to talk to your father, I say.

He's eating, she says, and she shows me her own ring, something she probably got with gumballs.

I need to see him now, I say. It's an emergency.

What kind? she says.

The secret kind.

She frowns and leads me through their living room. Near their bathroom, I grab her shoulder and stop us and ask, You eat yet?

Just about to. Deer's meat from Norm Skoronek!

Don't eat that meat, I say.

Why not?

I can't say. It has to do with my emergency.

But I *love* deer's meat!

Don't eat it, I say, and we walk into the dining room, where Junie is sitting beside Bruno, who's ready-set to slice the eggbread. STOP! I yell at him, and he sees me and stops and elbows Junie. And that's what makes me know they've had whoopee—the way he elbows her, trying to hide it.

What's with the barging? his pa Pinky asks.

Hi, Paulie, Junie says to me with a new fake-gold-chunk necklace touching her bosom.

Hello, I say, and I don't know what to say next. I don't want to explain about the ring because I don't want Junie to know I bought it—and because Pinky bought the eggbread, so he might call the ring legally his.

I should've powdered, his wife Jo-Jo says.

Little Karen stabs a slice of rabbit off the platter.

This humidity, Jo-Jo says, makes my hair like a Brillo Pad.

Your hair's fine, I say. It's your eggbread you should worry about. I just got word from the flour company that the flour we use might contain industrial strength rat poison.

Little Karen sets the meat-slice on her plate—and the door bell rings. Get that, Karen, Jo-Jo says, and Little Karen rolls her eyes and runs off.

Probably Sophie, Junie tells Jo-Jo. I asked her to stop by to help us eat the you-know-what. She points her fork at a pile of stewed cabbage leaves beside the meat slices—where I bet underneath is the rabbit's carcass.

You're kidding, Jo-Jo says.

You wanted it eaten in one sitting, no? Junie says.

By us here, Jo-Jo says back. Not company who'll bad-mouth my hairstyle.

Little Karen returns with Sophie and Waju. Sophie's holding up her bandaged third finger as if she's giving us the bird.

Same to you, Pinky tells her, and, while she and he wink, everyone laughs—except me and Waju.

Doctor's orders is why she holds it like so, Waju says, but no one at the table seems to hear him.

Except Jo-Jo, who stands and crosses herself and leaves the room.

What's this about a diamond in this eggbread? Waju asks me.

A diamond? Pinky says.

Try *poison,* I say to Waju, and I hate the fact that I'm lying to my honest-to-goodness flesh and blood. Who told you diamond?

The Lutz girl, Waju says.

The Lutz girl is crazy, I say, and I realize I'm bad-mouthing the Lutz girl because of Junie's whoopee with Bruno.

You gave the LUTZ GIRL a DIAMOND? Junie asks me. She's leaning away from Bruno, and Bruno's gaping at her mouth, probably because he don't like the fact that she cares to yell at me after she's had the secret whoopee with him. Waju too is frowning, but at me—for ruining business by saying our flour is poisoned—and Sophie is still giving Pinky the finger, but they're smirking—because *they* made whoopee that night Waju was off against Hitler.

HUH? Junie says to me.

I face Little Karen, and she scrunches her nose at me and forks a piece of rabbit toward her mouth.

I'M ASKING A *QUESTION,* Junie says.

Little Karen's still scrunching; she bites the rabbit-piece off the fork, then chews and sticks out her tongue and giggles like she's beating the devil. If she swallows, I think, she'll be like her father and Sophie and Junie and Bruno—wanting and doing without caring about consequences—so I point and say, Spit that out.

She grins so that meat bulges through her two missing teeth there.

SPIT IT OUT! I yell.

He's nutso, Sophie says.

NOW! I yell louder.

Why? Little Karen asks, and she chews.

Because, I say quiet-like. You're eating a darned rabbit.

It's *deer's* meat, she says with her mouth full.

From Norm Skoronek, Pinky says.

I take a fork from Junie's hand and shove aside the cabbage slices—and there, baked brown, is the carcass.

Little Karen stops chewing. Staring at the carcass, everyone is, and I point out for them a few black and white hairs on one of the feet.

THAT'S MY TOODLES! Little Karen yells. She faces Pinky and spits the meat; it hits his forehead and falls to his lap. Then she runs from the table into Jo-Jo in the doorway.

MY *TOODLES!* she says with tears in the eyes, and Jo-Jo takes and hugs her head. DAD KILLED HIM!

Beside Waju, Sophie points her bandaged finger at me. Why did you have to tell her, Paulie?

Because sooner or later, Jo-Jo says, we all have to spit it out.

What-now? Pinky says.

At least you do, Jo-Jo says back to him.

As do you, Waju says to Sophie.

As do you, I say to Junie.

Bruno sits back and folds his arms. Blushing, he is—and ignoring me.

What are you talking about? Junie asks me.

You know, I say. And if you don't leave with me now to spit out what you know in private, I'll spit it out here for everyone.

He *is* nutso, she says to Sophie.

I know they don't think I'll actually explain, because cheaters count on the honest—like me and Waju and Jo-Jo—to look away or keep quiet. And I've been quiet, I realize, because being quiet is easier.

So I point at Junie's gold chunks and say, You've been making whoopee. I point to Bruno and say, With him.

Don't talk like that around Little Karen, Junie says.

YOU GIVE HIM REASON, Little Karen says to Junie. I SEEN YOU WITH BRUNO. I SEEN BOTH YOUR BARE ASSES IN DAD'S FORD WHEN I USED TO GO OUT TO FEED TOODLES.

Bruno covers his eyes with his hand.

AND THAT'S WHY YOU KILLED TOODLES! Little Karen screams at Pinky. BECAUSE YOU DIDN'T WANT ME SEEING THEIR BARE ASSES WHEN I WENT TO FEED!

And I saw your ass, I say to Pinky. With Sophie.

Waju glares at Sophie.

Your brother's nutso, she tells him.

I don't think so, he says.

You're nutso, Sophie tells him. It runs in your family.

You think I never suspected? Waju asks her. After all these years of your Pinky-winks?

You made time with Sophie? Jo-Jo asks Pinky.

Pinky don't say a thing. He shakes his head. Then he sighs. Yeah, but before we were married, he says. *Years* before.

During the war? Waju asks Sophie.

Sophie don't answer, just blinks, chewing gum.

While we were engaged? Waju asks her.

She stares at her bandaged finger.

Huh? Waju says.

These stitches, she says, are making me faint. I gotta go, she says, and she walks out the room toward the front door.

Bull *crap*, Waju yells, and he grabs the eggbread off the table and follows her, and I think of chewing out Bruno but instead follow Waju, and the sound of Junie's fake-gold necklace chunks follows me.

Where you going? I ask her over my shoulder in the living room.

To apologize, she says.

Apologize to Bruno, I say, and I open the front door and walk out and close it, but she follows me out, where Waju is getting into his Rambler. He closes the door against Sophie on the street, then locks it and locks the others. I'm nearing the Rambler and they're both staring ahead, Waju through the windshield, Sophie at her tight white adhesive, and then Junie, behind me, says, Stop.

She grabs the back of my shirt and stops, so it's either let the shirt tear or hear lies, so I walk faster and my buttons pop and the back of the shirt tears and Junie lets go. Waju and Sophie ignore me as I pass the Rambler, and then I'm ahead of everyone. I want to turn and get in the car with Waju and tell him he and I should ride off alone, but his business is his business— and if I turned, Junie would think I turned for her.

At the end of the block, the necklace sounds no longer follow, so I slow down. I pass bungalow after bungalow, each one shut and painted nice, no extra stories or eggbreads or rabbit hutches or diamonds anywhere, just sprinklers going in front of the chairs on the porches. Some of the chairs have on them couples old enough to be grandparents, and some of the couples smoke Chesterfields and others drink from insulated tumblers, and none of them argue, just nod at me and watch their sprinklers hit their sidewalks and lawns and geraniums.

Then I hear brakes like Waju's squeaking beside me. Sophie's with him, I think, and they'll end up together, and together in their silence they'll hate me. The Rambler pulls even and inside is Waju alone, and he waves me over and points to the passenger seat.

So I stop. And get in. The eggbread he took from the table is on the dash, and he don't say anything. Neither do I, and he drives toward the bakery, but halfway there, a few doors before St. Josaphat's, he pulls over, and we sit.

He takes the eggbread off the dash, breaks it in half, and hands one to me. I figure he wants us tear our halves again and again into halves until we either find the diamond or don't, but he sits holding his half and stares out the windshield.

Then he lifts his half, takes a bite from it, and chews.

And I do the same.

Kid almost swallowed that rabbit, he says, chewing.

Woulda gone right down the tubes, I say.

Then we both sit and chew, looking ahead.

Pocket

*T*o be honest I don't know exactly when Pocket moved in here. All I remember is waking up one Saturday and going downstairs to take a piss and seeing a flat-headed dude with his jacket still on passed out face-down on our living room couch. His one arm hung over the side of the couch, and his fingers were so close to a pair of them aviator glasses on the floor you could hardly have slid a razor blade between there. I was walking past him when he took a deep breath through his nose and lifted that flat-backed head and saw me, the skin on his forehead looking like a waffle from the upholstery on the couch. We both pretended he didn't see me, he went back to sleep, and I went to take the piss.

When I got up for good that afternoon I'd forgotten all about him; I didn't remember him until the next afternoon, when a phone rang in our basement. Which at first I thought was from the TV, because we didn't have a phone. Then it rang again and Conekoff told me that there was a dude named Pocket living in the basement who put a phone in, paid all those deposits and hook-up fees and everything. Only we couldn't use it unless we asked him.

I asked Conekoff why they called this guy Pocket. He said Pocket wouldn't say. I asked why Pocket was living in the basement when there was an empty room upstairs. He said something about Pocket wanting privacy, and right away I figured Pocket gay. Then Conekoff told me a story I sometimes like to remember.

He said that Pocket used to go to college. Said Pocket was taking this test and had some formulas written on the palm of his hand but ended up not needing them and forgot they were there and couldn't read a mimeographed test question, so he raised his hand and the professor saw the formulas. Professor says, Let's see that. Pocket clenches his fist. Professor grabs Pocket's wrist and says, Let's see. Pocket says, right in front of the whole college class, You're not seeing anything inside this fist, just stars inside your head if you don't let go my goddamn arm. Professor says, Let's go visit the Dean. Pocket says, Let go. Professor doesn't let go, so Pocket makes a fist with his clean hand and lets the professor have one on the jaw, and the professor's lit pipe flies across the room and lands in some smart fat girl's lap. Right on the crotch. Next day Pocket gets kicked out of college for hitting a professor in front of a whole college class, and for cheating.

Now for that first couple weeks there, neither Conekoff or me hardly heard or saw a sign of Pocket. Just his phone ringing and the bright yellow piss he left in the can. Then, just like that, Conekoff up and went to Minnesota, where, I heard later, he married a dancer with scorpions tattooed on her neck.

For a week or so after Conekoff left I felt pretty alone here, even though that basement phone always rang at dinnertime and Pocket was always down there to answer it.

Then one night I was sitting on the living room couch and there was this bang on the door. I turned around and looked and Pocket exploded in, red-faced drunk. His eyebrows were black as charcoal and thick as my thumb and slanted down toward his nose, which was shaped like a baby's. I never saw a nose like that on anyone that big—Pocket probably went six-four, two-thirty. I guess our conversation got rolling after I asked him why they called him Pocket. Which made his face scrunch drunker.

Because that's what I was, he finally said.

I felt so stupid for not knowing what he meant that I couldn't look him in the eye.

Used to bet pro football in college, he said. Big. Through a book and everything. Always won, too. So when my buddies lost and doubled up and lost again and needed money to keep the book from playing wishbone with their legs, I'd have it.

So *Pocket,* I thought.

Had so much dough one night after squareup I rolled a joint with a dime bag of sense and a hundred dollar bill, Pocket said. Smoked it down to right between Ben Franklin's eyes and gave the rest to my buddies.

I started loading my ceramic Buddha-shaped bong, but Pocket took off his aviator glasses and laid face down on the floor, so I just sat there looking at his flat-backed head, to let him crash. But he kept talking.

Finally lost big one night, he said into the floor. Betting hoops. Took the points against Army and some bowlegged jarhead prayed in a buzzer jumper to bump the lead from eighteen to twenty, with the line at eighteen and a hook.

Shit, I said, even though I didn't know how pointspreads worked back then.

Two grand plus grease, Pocket said. So then I double up on a West Coast pro game and watch the Sonics cream me on cable. After that I quit.

Quit, I said. Betting's nothing I ever did enough to not do and call it quitting, I said.

Yeah, quit, Pocket said. Worked a nightwatchman job at that Josslyn Art Museum to pay it off. Was four grand plus change in debt but they trusted me with all those expensive paintings because I was in college. A year later, I bet once more. Just twenty bucks. Another game right on the number the whole fourth quarter, just like that Army game. Lost by a free throw.

Sonofabitch, I said.

Decided at the buzzer that gambling is either real stupid or real smart, depending on which side you're on.

Got a point there.

And since every bettor ends up dumping sooner or later, the smart side is booking. So I start keeping my buddies' bets rather than calling them in for them. Took a lot of money from them that way, 'cause if they ever won big I'd just tell them I didn't get a hold of the book. Still lent them ammo when they were down, though. 'Cause they were friends.

Ammo? I said.

Green, Pocket said. *Cash.*

So they still called you Pocket, I said.

Until one of them found my tally sheet, Pocket said. Fell out of my pocket in the dorm shitter. After that they called me lots of things. 'Cause they weren't friends anymore. Just bettors.

Pretty soon every night round suppertime Pocket and I would be in his basement bedroom, him running his business from his kid-sized desk, me laying on his bed listening.

Don't have the numbers yet, Pocket would say if anyone called before five. What's your figure? I got plus two ten. Two six*teen?* You're wrong, pal. Add again, call me later.

Bang, the phone would go.

Cockeater can't even add right, Pocket would say.

Ring.

Yeah, Pocket would say. Theresa. Let me call you later. Yeah. *Bang.*

Theresa was one of Pocket's women, which he had lots of. Never got those women mixed up, though. Not even on the phone.

Learn voices real quick in this business, he once told me. *Have* to.

So all his women, Jane and Val and Theresa and Sue and the rest, used to think they were his girlfriend. Just like Pocket hoped he was Jane's boyfriend. Which he wasn't. Which he knew. Jane's boyfriend was some businessman who was always out of town on weekdays.

With women, Pocket always said, you don't wanna be the fave. Too easy to get upset. You wanna be the dog.

Said that one night just before the phone rang.

Yeah, Pocket said into the phone; I was laying on his made bed with my hands under my head and my elbows sticking out, thinking about who I'd bet. Until Pocket started yelling.

I got sixty-odd college tilts, he yelled at the bettor, nine pro with over-unders, a caller on each ear, and you want me to repeat a Murray *State* spread? You better not be middlin' me, pal. It's six. No. Five. It's five. And put a hook on everything. *Bang.*

Sonofabitch drilled me a new asshole last week, Pocket told me. Took me for two grand. You just know he's middlin' me.

You don't have no caller on each ear, I said.

I know, Pocket said.

Then why you say you do?

So they think I'm big. They think I'm big and they bet big. They bet big and they lose big.

And if they win big?

These stiffs won't. Not for very long, at least. And if they do, I've got the kitty pretty well built up.

Kitty? I said.

A safety deposit box down at that Savings and Loan on Farnham, Pocket said. Keep everything I make in there except for what I need to live on. You know. Beer. And food.

You mean them eggs and that orange flavored water you keep in the fridge?

Yeah. Beer and that. And vitamins.

Ring.

Yeah, Pocket said into the phone. Yeah. That's four *forty*. Say 'em with the grease figured in. Three and a *hook*. Anything else? *Bang.*

What was I saying? Pocket asked me.

Something about vitamins.

Vitamins? Oh yeah. My kitty.

Pocket leaned his chair back to get something from his front pants pocket.

See this? he said.

Do I look like Helen Keller? I said.

Want me to answer that like an honest man? he said smiling, and then he leaned toward me. He held a tiny copper-colored key between his finger and thumb.

To the kitty? I said.

Yeah, Pocket said. I wanted you to know in case I ever get busted and need bail money. Someone'll have to run to the Savings and Loan, and I'd rather not have it be some lawyer.

Why no lawyer?

Can't trust those bastards. A lot of my college buddies were studying to be mouthpieces.

How am I supposed to get bail when the kitty key's in jail with you? I asked.

It won't *be* in jail with me, Pocket said. It'll be here, he said. And he put the key under the left back leg of his kid-sized desk. I only have it on me around squareup, he said.

And if you get busted on squareup?

I'll call you, Pocket said.

With your one phone call.

Yeah. And don't try anything smart, 'cause we're the only two that know about that kitty and I keep track of the total. And you know what I did to that professor.

Pocket smiled, and I did too.

How much is in there? I said.

Never enough, Pocket said. But getting there. Maybe ten grand. He held his thumb real close to his dialing finger. That's only this much in hundreds, he said.

Then he got up and walked over to the busted wash machine and reached in and pulled out one of them big yellow envelopes.

See *this?* he asked.

Yeah, I said.

Now this is sealed, so don't go looking in it, but I want you to give this to the old boy if anything ever happens to me.

I was ready to ask him what he meant by that when I figured it out.

What's in it? I said instead.

A few things I wrote, Pocket said. To the old boy. See the old boy used to play nosetackle for Iowa.

A Hawkeye, I said.

And he wanted me to play college ball like him.

You never played?

In high school I did. But not in college. Too slow, the scouts said. Won all these trophies, had my name in the paper a thousand times for high school, but I was too slow for college.

So you never played.

Not in college. They can fix small in the weight room, but there's nothing they can do about slow.

Plain bad luck, I said.

You got it. Went to college anyway, though. On the old boy's savings.

And then you got thrown out for hitting that professor.

And the old boy hasn't talked to me since.

So you got the last word in. In that envelope.

I wouldn't call it that.

You got one of them kitty keys in there?

No. Can't duplicate those keys.

You got a note telling him what to do with the kitty key?

Why you asking all these questions? Pocket said. He smiled, and I did too. The only way you're getting ammo from that kitty is if it's my bail money, Pocket said. Or if you bet lucky. You still like the Sixers tonight?

How many you giving? I said.

Got them at a pick, Pocket said, and he looked at me real serious.

The *Trib* had them getting three, I said.

Ring.

Yeah, Pocket said into the phone, and when he got to yelling at the bettor I got to staring at the pipes on our basement ceiling, trying to figure out the smart side of the Sixers at a pick.

Put twenty on the Sixers that night. They dumped by one, which meant that if Pocket had gave me the newspaper line, I would've hit. Which was a forty dollar swing, plus grease.

Next night I was kinda mad at Pocket for dicking with the line, but we still talked and joked like friends. I doubled up on the Sixers and they dumped again, which I couldn't believe, and which put me down forty-four.

Next day I didn't bet. Or eat. The only cash I had was thirty-some dollars, with squareup coming up a good week and a half before my next unemployment check.

Next night the Sixers played the Celtics; this time I bet against the Sixers 'cause it was at the Garden. Got so nervous before the news came on that night I couldn't eat, which was good because the Sixers beat Boston on the board, and which put me down eighty-eight.

I don't even want to think about the next two days. All I have to say is that when you bet on a road team playing on cable, it's like eleven thousand idiots are in your living room cheering for you to lose money. And also that after them two days, I was minus two hundred some.

Next day I rode it all on the Lakers. They were ten point faves and not on cable so after a hit off my Buddha bong, I fell asleep on the couch until someone knocked on the door—I thought for sure it was Pocket coming home to get scores from the news.

But instead it was this red-haired Val chick I never seen before but who Pocket once told me how she looked naked, which he said was not as good as a black-haired girl.

Where's John? she said, which was Pocket's birth certificate name. He and I are supposed to go out tonight.

I don't know, I said, even though I knew he was out with Jane 'cause it was a weeknight and Jane's boyfriend the businessman was out of town.

You don't have to lie for him, she said. I know he's a book and that he's probably out collecting.

You're right, I said, which was another lie because squareup was the next day—which I knew because if the Lakers didn't cover that night, I'd have to pay up somehow.

Could I come in from the cold and have a cigarette and wait for him? Val said. We had a fight last night and I have to see him.

Yeah, I said a second before I meant it.

Someone hit a parlay for twelve grand on John last night, she said. I just want to make sure that's why he was pissed.

It's probably why, I said, even though I hadn't heard about no twelve grand. I figured the reason Pocket fought with Val was because Jane had just told him she wasn't sure she wanted to have a second boyfriend because she wanted to marry the out-of-town businessman.

Val sat on the chair across from me. She had a pretty face for cigarette smoking, and after she shook out her match I turned on the TV 'cause it was almost time for sports scores to come on. John talks about you a lot, she said when I sat back on the couch.

I didn't like hearing her say John instead of Pocket. The only other time anyone called him John was his phone bill when I brought in the mail. If it's good stuff, I said. It's lies.

Val didn't smile, just kept looking at me and smoking, and right then I remembered Pocket saying how it's best to be the dog with women.

The weather part of the news was on, and I started getting nervous about my Lakers bet. Val and I watched TV without talking and a commercial came on. Val crossed her one leg over the other and it started bouncing up and down fast. You want a beer? I finally said.

Sure, she said. She smiled, and I did too.

I never drank Pocket's beer but Val wasn't my woman—and I figured what the hell, if I can't think of anything to say, the least I can do is give her a beer. Only there were no Buds in the fridge, just Pocket's gallon of orange-flavored water and eggs. I found a couple clean glasses and poured the orange water, and Val watched me bring hers to her. There was a car commercial on TV. Sports was next.

All we got to drink is this, I said.

Looks like a winner, she said, her leg still bouncing, and she smiled again.

I sat down and pretended to watch the commercial. I knew she had it bad for Pocket, and that she probably felt like a dog around him because he liked Jane, and that this meant she probably wanted me—Conekoff once said that's the way women are and I could just feel him being right again.

I tried not to think about that, but there was nothing else to think about except that the orange flavored water tasted like the fridge smelled, and that I'd be seeing my Lakers score any minute.

Then the scores started rolling and I subtracted mine out in my head. I thought the Lakers covered by a free throw, but then I subtracted on a piece of paper and they'd won by nine, not the eleven I thought, so instead I *lost* by the free throw, which put me down over four hundred.

Sonofabitch, I said, and I remembered how Conekoff used to say that the problem with unemployment is that you can't work it for overtime. I also remembered the time Pocket told me to never double up when you're down big.

The thing was, Pocket knew I was down and booked me anyway.

I couldn't think of anything but the minus four hundred some; I didn't have the exact figure but I didn't want to pencil it out because I didn't have the money anyway.

Val asked when Pocket would be back from squareup, and I felt so sorry for her that I lied again, I said, Not for awhile, he went out with a buddy after squareup.

Does this buddy have a woman's name? Val said, her leg bouncing again.

I looked at her eyes and, right then, got real tired of lying for Pocket, so I said, Yeah. Jane.

Val's leg bounced faster, and then she asked where the bathroom was.

I took a hit off the Buddha bong while she was gone. When she came back, she sat on the couch next to me and did a bong hit herself. I thought about what Pocket said about the way she looked naked, and everything felt more quiet than it had been. Then I felt Val looking at me, so I looked at her. And then it happened. So quick I never even took my glasses off.

After we finished, when she was putting her first leg into her panties, she said, It's fine with me if tonight stays our little secret.

I thought through what Pocket meant about being a dog with women.

Well? Val said. She looked so stupid without her cigarette or anything, her legs bent out like a frog's when she snapped her panty elastic onto her waist, and even though it had felt better than I thought it would, now I had to think about getting some kind of infection, maybe the one Conekoff had the time I walked into our bathroom and he was taking a syringe to himself.

Well, I don't know, I said. If you don't mind, I think you should leave. Or did you want to stay for another one of them orange drinks.

You're *mad?* Val said.

Of course not, I said. Just tired.

You seemed a little nervous, she said. What, don't you screw very often?

I screw when I want, I said, which was a lie 'cause I hadn't done it for years before that, plus I'd just done it without really wanting to.

So are you gonna tell him? she asked.

I guess you'll find out, I said.

You're mad, she said.

Maybe you should just leave, I said.

Maybe, she said, and she lit another cigarette and left.

When Pocket came back that night, red-faced drunk as usual, we did a few hits off the Buddha, and he took off his glasses and put them and his change and wallet and stuff on the Salvation Army coffee table, which he always did before he laid down on the wood floor to bullshit with me.

As soon as he laid down I said, Guess what.

What, he said.

Guess, I said.

I don't know, Pocket said. The Lakers covered and you're back to even?

No, I said. The Lakers dumped. I owe you four something.

Why you sound like you're smiling then? Pocket asked.

'Cause it's kinda funny, I said. You know that redhead Val that's got it for you?

Yeah.

I made love on her.

You *what?* Pocket said, and he sat up and looked at me.

I made love on her.

Pocket's face turned redder. What you go and do something like that for? he said. I oughta beat the cream corn shit out of you, glasses and all.

What you so mad about? I said.

YOU FUCKED MY WOMAN! Pocket yelled, and he stood up and stared at me with those slanted eyebrows and his eyes misaligned like some kinda crazy goofcock.

She's not your woman, I said. You don't even like her.

I like her, Pocket said. I spend *money* on her.

You don't even like the way she looks naked, I said.

I think she looks *great* naked, Pocket said, kicking the coffee table so hard that a leg went flying under the TV and the Buddha did a swan dive into the floor, smashing into a million pieces that spread out like marbles from a busted bag.

I stared at the one piece of the Buddha next to my little toe while Pocket picked up his glasses and wallet and change from between the other pieces, and then I said to him, You're just pissed 'cause you lost twelve grand on that parlay last night. And tomorrow's squareup.

What are you talking about? Pocket said. I didn't lose no twelve grand. Where'd you get an idea like that?

Val, I said.

So you went ahead and plugged her, he said. He walked to the door and left without even closing it, and when he didn't come back I felt more alone than ever.

Next day was squareup, so I went downtown and pawned my clock radio for ten bucks so I could at least put a dent in what I owed Pocket. But Pocket didn't come home that day, or the next day or the day after that.

The day after *that* was Saturday. I was watching a Nebraska hoops game and was pissed because according to the Gold Sheet the Huskers were tough home dogs and I wanted to pile on them and win back my money, and now they were winning the game outright, but Pocket still wasn't home.

Right after halftime there was this knock on the door; I thought it was Pocket without his keys or something.

I opened the door and it was Val, her nose red and running and blowing white cigarette smoke into the cold.

Where's John, she said.

Out, I said.

When's the last time you saw him? she said.

Few days ago.

He say where he was going? she asked. And then I saw the newspaper under her arm, and that she was shivering, and that her eyes were red, too, not just her nose.

No, I said.

She took the newspaper from under her arm and started unfolding it with her cigarette between her fingers. You see this? she said.

She was unfolding the section with the weather map on it, and I only read the Sports, so I said, No.

She held the paper in front of my face and pointed to this article about this guy's body they found in a hefty bag in the trunk of a car after a police wrecker had taken it to one of them impounding lots. The guy's head had a bullet in it and the cops didn't know who he was.

I think this might be John, Val said, real nervous-like.

You're crazy, I said.

He owed a lot of money, she said. For a long time. He told me that.

He never told me that, I said.

You never slept with him, she said.

He's my best friend, I said.

He's your only friend, she said.

You're crazy, I said. You just want me to make love on you again. Why don't you just leave.

I'm being serious here, Val said, and her eyes almost looked like it but not enough for me to believe her. I really think it was John, she said.

Then do the cops a favor and identify him.

I can't. I have a boyfriend and everything. I thought you might identify him. You being his roommate and all.

I don't think that was him in the hefty bag, I said. I think he's gone 'cause he's pissed at me for making love on you.

It says here, Val said, that the victim was twenty-five to thirty years old and was dead for a little over forty-eight hours. That sounds too much like John for me to ignore it.

Right then I remembered hearing about a girl they found naked and dead in Kearney but they couldn't identify her or tell if she was raped because buzzards had got to her before the search party did. And suddenly everything felt real different. Then I remembered Conekoff telling me that women will do just about anything to sleep with a guy if they have their mind set on it, so I said to Val, You just want me to make love on you again. And that's the reason he's gone in the first place.

Why would I want to do that again? she said.

'Cause you're crazy, I said, and Val left crying.

Next Tuesday I was sure Pocket would be back any day. I was leaving the house to go to the Seven Eleven when this Buick pulled up, with Iowa plates. An old man and an old lady got out, and just when I reached the sidewalk the old lady said to me, Is this where John Tilleson lived?

I looked at her real close. She had that same baby's nose that Pocket had, so I said, Yes, ma'am. You're his mother?

She looked me in the eye when she nodded and she wasn't crying or anything—in fact she looked kinda mad—so I told myself that Val was paranoid about that hefty bag deal and that Pocket had just gone home to his parents.

We came to get his stuff, she said. If you don't mind.

Not at all, I said. And then I thought to myself, She's so calm Pocket can't be dead. And that made me shiver.

Pocket's dad looked at the yard and wobbled from side to side as we walked up the porch stairs; he didn't have very broad shoulders for a Big Ten nosetackle but then again guys his age don't lift weights and he was probably a quick sonofabitch when he played for Iowa. From the way things looked, if Pocket got his size from anyone, it was his ma.

We walked through the living room past the coffee table Pocket kicked the last time I saw him—it was wobbly even though I used Superglue to put that leg back on.

I led them into the basement, and when we were all down there Pocket's ma started taking the sheets off his bed as if she did that kinda thing every day. I watched her the whole time and she never looked ready to cry, not even once.

Then she went to the cardboard closet Pocket brought down from Conekoff's room after Conekoff left here, and took all his pants and shirts and things and hung them on Pocket's dad's arm, which he held straight out. With all them clothes on there, Pocket's dad looked a lot stronger than I first thought.

Then Pocket's ma pulled a big baggie from her purse and stuffed all of Pocket's underwear and socks in it, and when she was done with that I was staring at the storm window Pocket fixed when he moved in, and I felt sad, not because I thought Pocket was dead, but because living with his parents in Iowa might be worse than dead, with the same chance of him ever coming back.

I was looking at that window when Pocket's dad started making these crying sounds.

I told myself that he was crying because Pocket had been busted, not because he was the guy in the hefty bag. But then Pocket's dad said, with his voice real high, Do you have any idea why? And he was looking at me.

It wasn't easy watching an old ballplayer wipe his red face with his handkerchief, so I looked back at the storm window and shook my head no, and everything felt real different all of a sudden, like midnight on New Year's Eve, but backwards. And worse. Everything even *looked* different.

When Pocket's ma and dad started walking to the stairs, I said, Wait.

I went to the busted wash machine and got the yellow envelope and gave it to Pocket's dad, in his free hand.

John told me to give this to you, I said, and I probably would've started crying right then if I'd have called him Pocket.

What is it? Pocket's ma said.

Pocket's dad managed to open the envelope, and he started reading a letter in Pocket's handwriting, which was all that was in there. Right then I remembered the kitty key and the ten grand and I thought, Maybe they killed him 'cause he refused to pay. I wanted Pocket's ma and dad to leave so I could see if the key was under the desk leg, which made me feel guilty.

He just told me to give that to his dad, I said to Pocket's ma. If something happened.

Then Pocket's clothes slid off Pocket's dad's arm and Pocket's dad hunched over and pulled his handkerchief back out and started crying even louder.

Let's go, honey, Pocket's ma said. Honey. She looked at me and I picked up the clothes and she led Pocket's dad by the hand up the stairs and out of the house. She said goodbye for both of them as I put the clothes in the back seat of the Buick, which Pocket's ma drove as they took off.

As soon as their Iowa plates disappeared around the corner I ran back inside and down the basement stairs and looked under that left back desk leg for the kitty key, feeling guilty and lucky at the same time. Only it wasn't there. I looked under all the desk legs to make sure and it wasn't under any of them or anywhere else around there. Then I thought it out. What made the most sense was that Pocket used the kitty key to pay off his bettors that squareup day after I last saw him, but the ten grand wasn't enough for someone not to shoot him.

Now everything felt even more different, so I went upstairs and smoked a joint and a half of sense and laid down on the couch with my hands under my head and my elbows sticking out, like I used to on Pocket's bed while he took calls. I thought about the four hundred some I owed him and how that bullet in his head brought me back to even, which again made me feel guilty and lucky at the same time, and then I fell asleep.

When I opened my eyes I was face-down against the couch's damn upholstery, my arm hanging over the side, my fingers almost touching a piece of the Buddha bong I must have missed when I swept up the day after Pocket left.

That piece of the Buddha made me remember how Pocket kicked the table right before I saw his flat-backed head leave here for the last time, which made me remember why he kicked the table, which made me remember making love on that stupid redhead Val, which happened just because someone missed a free throw in that damn Lakers game.

When my eyes focused better, I saw that the piece of the Buddha was part of a pile of stuff you always see under couches, it looked like dust and some hair and a penny. A penny from Pocket's change he kicked off the coffee table, I thought, and I stretched my arm to pick it up. Like him having this penny in his pocket would have kept that bullet from his head when his kitty wasn't enough, I thought.

Only when I picked it up it wasn't a penny. It was a key, tiny and copper-colored, and pretty soon warm and sweaty, 'cause I was holding it between my finger and thumb like Pocket used to, back when he did the booking and I was broke and stupid about pointspreads.

Unknown Rook

Y ou gotta hear this, Burk—listen to this. I'm at spring training, right? No, CACTUS League. Arizona, Burk. Chandler. Near Phoenix. I've become an A's fan since I moved—Huh? SCREW the Yankees. Anyway listen to this, Burk. LISTEN.

I had three weeks' vacation time? You know, use it or lose it? So I go to Chandler. This was last year—no, *two* years ago. And the A's had this kid, this rook outfielder, not Canseco's brother but some other kid who still hasn't panned out—I forget his name, Burk. Anyway, it's *ninety* out, Burk; it's freaking March and it's *ninety*, so I get up early—see I'm staying at this Motel Six, and I open the drapes and see WOMEN, Burk, young ones, three-quarters-naked butt cheeks lying all over this astroturf pool deck like billiard balls on green pool table felt. So I go out there to mark up my racing form, and in half an hour I'm sunburned, and I go to Turf Paradise, hit a few wins on the nose, walk out forty ahead and head to the ballyard. Huh?

I forget the name of the place, but it's in Chandler, Burk—you gotta drive a little from town, but you pop a Miller on the way and its worth it, so I get there—Huh?

YEAH I was alone, and it was Oakland against someone shitty, I can't remember—WAS it the Cubs? It doesn't matter; what matters is it was ninety and there were no clouds in the sky—and this in MARCH.

So I buy my ticket and I go into the park, halter tops and shorts everywhere—Burk, you can smell the Coppertone cocoa butter in the air, and everyone's red, Burk, red for the first time that year, and they're all smiles. And I'm so happy I don't care that I'm three innings late, and I decide to fight the crowd by sitting in the upper grand.

No, not at all as a high as a major league upper grand but the second section up of these bleachers, right? You know, with a whole section of bleachers below me?

So I'm up there looking down, and there's all this pink and brown skin, Burk, all this tight, gleaming skin everywhere, and white smiles and green and gold and blue and red T-shirts—I guess it WAS the Cubs they were playing, Burk. Anyway I'm looking down at it all and thinking, God damn, am I glad I got outta that pregnancy mess with Tricia. Huh?

Of course I was still ALONE, Burk. But I'm not minding that at all. In fact, I'm ENJOYing it, because, well, there are women everywhere; if I look down to my left I can see this one—the svelte type, you know what I'm saying? Svelte and about our age, maybe younger, frosted hair—you know the type. She's got on one of those, you know, what do you call them?—tube tops?—and after the A half of the fifth she slides the thing down off her right ... TIT ... and this kid, this BABY, starts sucking. Beautiful tit, too, and what's best is I got a perfect angle to watch.

So I'm sitting there pounding these twenty-two ounce beers, watching the kid suckle and the players playing and the freaking palm trees around Camelback Mountain, and I think, God DAMN, this is America. And then the A's come up and the woman with the tit grabs the kid by the back of the head and pulls his little suction cup lips off her nipple, then pulls some baby oil out of this diaper bag and rubs the stuff over her shoulders and most of the tit—and she's right out there in the CROWD, Burk. No—NO ONE else sees it 'cause I'm the only one in the upper section and she's down on the highest bleacher in the section below me and everyone in her section is watching the freaking GAME.

So I'm sitting there staring—Christ, a foul ball could have hit me between the eyes and I wouldn't have known—and she puts it back—the tit

I mean—and lays the kid on this little blue blanket beside her and covers him with it; you know, you don't wanna broil the little sucker.

And then they announce this rook, Burk. I forget the guy's name but he's in the A's system, or at least was—maybe he WAS non-roster—and the crowd goes freaking APE. Everyone's cheering Burk; I've never heard of this guy before but they're all cheering, and I'm thinking, Is this guy the son of some Hall of Famer or WHAT?

His name was Woods or Woodson or Somethingson—shit, I don't remember, but everyone there is screaming for him; all I could figure is that the guy's got his whole freaking family down there, right? You know, this family is screaming and everyone ELSE is screaming 'cause they HEAR screaming and they're half in the bag and it's March and it's freaking ninety out?

So whoever this rook is steps in, and this Double A vet from the Cubs, a lefty, submarines a fastball, grooves it low, and—POW!—the rook hits it, a CANNONball, Burk—freakin' frozen rope to the fence; centerfielder doesn't even jump, just pivots and puts his hands on his hips, watching this beeline that looks like it's going out on the rise, and the crowd goes bonkers immediately: everyone is standing before the rook reaches second, and I'm thinking homerun all the way, but the ball hits the wall and caroms back toward the infield, and this kid, this rook—you KNOW his eyes are big as quarters—is running like he's thinking triple, but the ball caroms back so hard the centerfielder picks it up easy and zings it over to third before the rook's even CLOSE.

So the rook puts on the brakes and heads back to second, but the shortstop's got it covered; the rook fakes a headfirst slide and then just stops and runs *backwards* to third, Burk, wheeling it full speed to third backwards. Turns into the longest pickle I ever seen, Burk, EVERY—FREAKING—GUY on the field touches the ball, the rook last—when he gets tagged at second by the CATCHER, and then this catcher DROPS the ball, and the rook's on the bag, and the ump thumbs him out, then signals safe. And then there's a beef, Burk; the other manager comes out and does the jaw-to-jaw arguing

37

with the ump, and they both do the in-your-face pointing until the manager frisbees his Skoal tin at the backstop; the crowd's still nuts, everyone still standing and screaming, and I'm buzzed but suddenly shaky, so I sit down. I notice my friend the svelte mother; she's standing and cheering, and her ass is unbelievable, Burk—a PEAR if there ever was one in clothes: I can't WAIT for her to sit down so I can see that tit again, and all of a sudden I think, Where's her goddamn KID?

I look on both sides of her, then down around her feet, and then way down—remember, she's on the highest bleacher in that section below me, so I'm looking WAY down behind her, and I see the blue blanket balled up on the GROUND, Burk—on the asphalt fifty feet below her. I can't see the kid in it but can't see him anywhere else either, and his ma isn't holding him; she's sipping a beer, standing and watching the ump and manager argue.

Then this guy, Burk—this guy with a cardboard tray of beers walking out from the concession area beneath everyone—STEPS on the blanket and stops walking just past it, and turns around and toes it with his sandal, then looks around—and, see, everyone is still cheering about the shit on the field—and walks off.

Then another guy—with his hands full of hotdogs—almost trips on the thing; he puts two hotdogs under his arm and stoops and opens the blanket, and I see a flash of pink skin. He closes the blanket and the crowd cheers louder; he runs to an old usher at the turnstile, taps him on the shoulder and brings him over, and the usher opens the blanket and stoops down and closes it, then scoops it up and lifts it, holding it out away from him like he's delivering a freaking PIZZA.

Huh? No. The woman is still standing and sipping and watching, facing the field like everyone else in the crowd, and for some reason the crowd starts laughing, and the usher's holding the kid out like that and looking up at the edge of the bleachers and yelling until this old lady toward the end of that highest row in that section looks down. The usher gestures the kid toward her, and she shakes her head no and looks back out at the field, and now the crowd's booing, and the usher's mouth is still moving—the guy's yelling his tonsils out—and this old lady looks down again and then turns around and says something to the guy beside her. And HE looks down and sees the kid and shakes his head, and then he taps the shoulder of this woman beside him, and the message goes down the row like that—until pretty much everyone on the top of that section is looking down at the blanket except for the kid's freaking mom.

Finally she sees people in front of her turning around, and this guy with binoculars beside her grabs her elbow, and she looks down beside her, then down at the other side, then way down at the usher, and she sees. She puts down her beer, covers her mouth with her hands, and just stands there, Burk. And all of us watching her are standing there staring at her the same way she's staring at her kid—as if we'd come there with her—our hands over our mouths, none of our lips moving to say one word, because there's nothing in Arizona that anyone can say—nothing in America, for Christ sake—and no one who knows what they've just witnessed wants to make eye contact with anyone else alive; I mean, for a week after I saw that—and this is no bull—I couldn't have looked in a mirror if you paid me a major league salary.

3 x 5 Steve

*K*ate sang. She sang in the shower, in the sack, and quietly down the aisles of her favorite used bookstore.

She did not sing quietly in the sack. She left for the Bay Area on May 24. I don't remember which year exactly: the end of that decade comes back to me now as a blur. I do remember sitting on my kitchen table the morning she left, reading my tiny checkbook calendar with her magnifying glass, seeing that May 24 was the day I would remember as the day the singing stopped.

On May 23, in her favorite used bookstore, she'd met a guy with a mustache who told her he'd help her make a Top Forty record in The Bay Area. And that in the meantime she could sleep on his Bay Area couch.

She left the next morning with a Schlitz sixpack hangover and red ribbons in her hair, eyes bloodshot but bulging with hope.

I haven't heard her voice since. I haven't heard her Top Forty record on my car stereo, which I listen to as God does the daily prayers of children.

■ ■ ■

On May 25 I browsed through Kate's favorite used bookstore. The place had that aura of Communism that for years had helped sell books to smarties. I was between aisles when I heard a voice:

"Looking for something specific?"

It had not spoken in melody. It belonged to a guy wearing a honey-gold beard and a coffee-stained T-shirt that fit like a condom. He had a PhD's squint and could have used a little sun. Make that a lot of sun.

He was the bookstore proprietor.

"Nothing specific," I answered.

He gave me the bookstore proprietor look: *I know you want something specific.* He walked away in Birkenstock silence. I browsed on. Still May 25, I thought. I browsed to the end of an aisle, where he'd provided his book buyers with free coffee and a cork board for their capitalistic dirty work.

The coffee was so free it had gotten up and left. But the cork board was crowded, a marketplace of recycled paper scraps:

HERB GARDEN STARTER KIT.
INCLUDES BASIL.
$195.00. 873-5564.

THIRD WORLD SANDALS.
* $65.00
* PROFITS GO TO THE HUNGRY
* 1-800-MGHANDI

I wondered whether the proprietor got a cut for providing the cork board. I wanted some coffee. Then a red scrap of paper begged me to read:

USED CAR STEREOS.
FROM BAY AREA.
$25 INSTALLED.
555-6969, AFTER 3.

Bay Area, I thought. I committed the number to memory, no difficult task. The proprietor's eyes, I sensed, were on me. I browsed to the bargain table near the front door, flipped through a *Das Kapital* to keep his sophisticated mind on its toes. I pivoted. "Where'd you get your sandals?" I asked.

He faced his sandals as if they were corporate attorneys.

"The Bay Area," he said.

Bay Area *again,* I thought. I looked him in the eye. "I really enjoy the Bay Area."

He gave me a little nod. "The Bay Area is excellent." He pursed his eyebrows as if he needed me to continue conversing. If I'd say the right thing, we'd be friends. I'd be able to walk into his bookstore without being hit by his look. I'd drink his free coffee.

"You ever buy a used car stereo?" I said.

His face soured. He consulted his sandals. To them my question was probably cake compared to their most important concern: the profitability of the aura of Communism now that The Wall was pieces of concrete auctioned to tourists.

He cleared his throat: the sandals must have given him the nod. "Do you mean a stereo for a used car?" he asked. "Or a used stereo for any car?"

I offered my most polite smile. "Either."

"No, sir," he said. "I have never bought a used car stereo."

■ ■ ■

Like an old high school librarian, I have always had a thing for 3 x 5 cards. I keep my working supply behind the calendar page of my checkbook, in the blue vinyl wallet mailed to me by a carpeted bank that makes me feel safe and American.

The first thing I did when I returned home from the used bookstore was consult that wallet for a card. I found the wallet in seconds, but my 3 x 5 cards, like all but $25 of my life's earnings, were gone. I fingered sweat off my forehead, headed straight for the basement of my apartment building, a demilitarized zone of snow tires, spider webs and rolled carpet remnants. Inside a Firestone snow tire was a good friend, my J. C. Penney shoebox. I opened J. C. and saw relief: four inches deep of 3 x 5 reliability.

I kissed the top card, took twenty, returned the shoebox to the snow tire. I remembered and wrote down the number for the Bay Area used car stereos, and felt hope for the rest of the day.

■　■　■

The phone number safe on the 3 x 5 card and deep in my pocket, I ate canned sardines on saltines and watched an important televised golf tournament.

The golf course was not in the Bay Area. It was in Georgia, where golfing appears natural as singing itself.

I watched golf with the sound off until 3:00. Then I grabbed my immobile phone, once a monument to Kate's voice.

While dialing I pictured her prone on that Bay Area couch.

"Hello?" the voice said.

It had not spoken in melody, but it had sounded female.

"Yes, ma'am," I said. "I'm calling about the used car stereo?"

"This ain't a ma'am, sir."

"Oh. Sorry. I'm calling about the used car stereo?"

"Come by after second shift. That's when the guy sells them."

I'd once worked second shift, doing factory maintenance. I had to climb a fifty-foot ladder every morning and dust one of two 50,000 volt electrical transformers with a red rag. And *not* dust the other one. The foreman holding the ladder would wear thick rubber gloves.

"What do you say I come around at about midnight?" I asked.

"Too early."

"How about one?"

"Three's as early as he'll sell."

Why *three?* I thought. And the voice still sounded female. The conversation wasn't making sense: the voice very well might have been Kate's.

"Still interested?" it asked.

That was a tough one. "Of course."

"Then let me give you the address. You got paper?"

"Yes, sir," I said, and I smiled, somewhat because I felt onto Kate's trail, mostly because I had my 3 x 5 card. I pulled it out of my pocket. Maybe, I thought, I don't need Kate. I felt OK about that.

■ ■ ■

My alarm clock sounded as loud as a siren. I slapped it off wondering where Kate was. Almost three in the morning, I thought, and I'm still wearing pants?

Then everything made sense. Kate was two days behind me.

Time to buy a used car stereo.

I drove quickly. I-80 had very little traffic. Then again it was three in the morning. I pulled my warm 3 x 5 card from my pocket, and the directions took me past some rowhouses, a railyard yard, a church. Then I saw the sign for Bartlett Street. I turned. Bartlett was an average American block, with trees, porches and duplexes. Well, maybe a little below average. But I was there. A new place, with new people. Screw Kate. I got out of my car, slid a hand into a pocket. My 3 x 5 card, my $25 in cash—they were there, too.

I knocked on a door facing the porch. No one answered. I saw a second door. It opened without me knocking, and then I was in the duplex's correct half. Two women sat on folding chairs. One was fat. The other was fatter. A coffee table sat between them without coffee, just twenty or so green ju-ju spearmint leaves piled into a cut-crystal bowl.

Those spearmint leaves didn't have a chance.

Two guys sat on a couch without cushions. The fatter woman wore jeans with the zipper half-down. She had a familiar look on her face: *Men owe me love regardless of my weight.*

I offered my newest polite nod, and a voice said, "You here to party?"

It had not spoken in melody. It had sounded female but had come from the couch. One of those guys is the guy who was on the phone, I thought. Or my new lady friend throws her voice.

"No," I said. "The last time I partied was 1976."

"What, you voted for Carter?" the fat woman said, and the room exploded with that loud kind of laughter fueled by draft beer and last-calls.

A tall child walked in and sat on a styrofoam cooler while the laughter made itself comfortable. He laughed also, but in the shy way of someone whose DNA was in the works in 1976.

He had a lifetime of weight-gaining ahead of him. The laughter stopped. "I'm here for the car stereo?" I said to a guy on the couch. He exchanged glances with his couchmate. They were both thin with thick black hair. They were one of those pairs of guys who first appear to be brothers, but then, after you give them the eye, don't even look like cousins.

The kid had red hair. Both women were fifteen-sixteenths blond. I hoped the kid's parents were pulling up out front, about to get him the hell out of there.

"We're partying now," one of the guys said. He snapped his fingers and the kid stood, opened the cooler and grabbed a can of Schlitz while finger-combing bangs from his eyes. He tossed the can across the room to me. *Schlitz,* I thought, and I dropped my 3 x 5 to catch the can against my chest. Then—dammit—I dropped the can.

The not-so-fat woman picked up my 3 x 5 card, put it on the coffee table. "You're gonna have yourself a foamy one there."

I picked up the can and nodded. Her soft eyes indicated she had a longer wick than her size 18 friend. Maybe they made a reasonable team.

I opened the can and foam sprayed everywhere. Every eye hit me—except the fatter woman's. She just sat, looking at her chest, breathing. She was braless and missing two blouse buttons, her breasts calm as udders. She wiped my Schlitz off her blouse, then smirked and reached for a spearmint leaf.

One of the two guys must have loved her.

"Sorry," I said, just in case.

"Don't sweat it," one of the guys said. The kid was staring at me, fingering his bangs.

"Have a seat," the other guy said. He was watching the fatter woman's zipper. "We'll talk stereos after we kill these sixers."

I sat on a stack of three couch cushions. The not-so-fat woman pulled a joint from a blond "sausage curl"—and for once the term made sense. She lit up, noticed me eyeing the joint, and frowned.

"What kinda wheels you drive?" the guy watching the fatter woman's zipper asked me.

"Ford."

"LTD?"

"Galaxie Five."

"Two door?"

"Four."

The guys looked at each other as if deciding whether to hire, rape or kill me. Their eyes did all the talking and the kid seemed to be reading their lips.

"That shouldn't be a problem," the guy who'd been watching the zipper said.

I didn't know what he was talking about. I sucked some Schlitz. "What shouldn't be a problem?"

Everyone sucked Schlitz, including the kid.

"Installing it," the guy who'd been watching the zipper said.

Then we sat drinking and smoking like a show business family. Actually we sat drinking while the not-so-fat woman smoked and everyone but me laughed. They'd laugh when one of them said something stupid. I'd fake smiles. Then the not-so-fat woman passed the joint to the kid, and they really laughed. The kid hit it good and crossed his eyes, and they laughed as if ghosts were taking feathers to them.

I didn't laugh. I didn't find a smoking kid funny. Smoking *monkeys* are funny, I thought. A kid is a kid. And now this one had smoked weed. Now he and his friends in six years wouldn't get kicks unless they robbed trucks. I didn't like what I was seeing. I was drinking Schlitz to insulate myself from the sight: the fall of a nation, a collapse worse than that of The Wall itself.

And Kate was practicing her hit song, perhaps on her back.

Hell, I thought. Smoking *monkeys* aren't funny.

"What's going on here?" a voice said.

It had had a sing-song quality. It belonged to someone walking up basement stairs leading to the room: a codger. The stairs were new to me. They'd been behind the fatter woman all along.

The codger was wearing a white paisley robe and blue vinyl slippers. His lips were as active as he was old, pursing and smacking while he stared at everything. He wore bifocals in the Old Man Tradition but looked trim and fit, his contribution to the honor left in the nation he'd fought for.

"Huh?" he said.

The kid and the not-so-fat woman looked at him. The guys looked at him. The fatter woman was breathing.

I looked at my Schlitz can, then, very calmly, at the codger.

Something about him was frightening. "I'm a whole floor below sleeping," he yelled. "And I wake up at three-thirty in the morning to the sound of all of yous *laughing?*"

These people don't know *Kate*, I thought—and the codger's bifocals locked themselves on my eyes.

"That's right, Gramps," the fatter woman said. "Laughing." She'd spoken too quietly for the codger, though. I glanced her way, to avoid my stare-down with him. She looked at her zipper and smirked.

"And *drinking?*" the codger said. His eyes stayed on mine. His lips smacked. "And *smoking?*"

The fatter woman slid two fingers between her open zipper flaps, craned her neck to aim her face in his direction. "What's a matter, old man? Aren't you getting enough fuckin'?"

That last word hit his face hard. He stood smacking his lips for four to five seconds.

"What?" he barely said.

The fatter woman craned her neck to make eye contact. "I *said*. Ain't. You. Getting. Enough. Fuckin'."

The kid smirked. The codger's lips smacked until his tongue settled them down. "Enough what?"

The fatter woman pushed her fingers deeper into her pants. "*Fuck*in'."

The codger reached into the breast pocket of his robe. He pulled out a pencil and a 3 x 5 card. I was behind him all the way on the 3 x 5 card. He centered it on his palm and aimed the pencil at a particular square millimeter, as if preparing to joust with a mosquito.

The pencil false-started. That pencil wanted action. His lips smacked until they came out with an ultimatum:

"Spell that."

The fatter woman looked at her not-so-fat friend, who tossed over a spearmint leaf. The fatter woman caught the spearmint leaf and held it in front of her mouth, eyes on her friend. "How do you spell *fuckin'?*" she asked.

"F-U-C," the not-so-fat woman said. She took the joint from the kid's mouth, toked it, spat a seed. "K-I-N."

The codger's pencil made contact. He wrote as slowly as a slug, as if he'd be graded on penmanship. When he finished, he stepped beside the fatter woman and held his 3 x 5 card in front of her face. "Is that what you said?" he asked.

I began liking the guy. She yanked the card from his fingers. She took longer to read it than he'd had to get it down.

"Yeah," she said, and she tossed the card over her head. It nicked the ceiling, then swooped smack into the styrofoam cooler. "And I'd like an answer," she said.

The codger walked to the cooler. The kid stepped back to the wall. The codger hitched up the thighs of his pajamas and squatted, keeping his spine perfectly straight. "Back problems," he told me. He reached into the cooler, pinched a corner of the card, pulled it out of the icewater.

"Have a malt liquor, Steve?" the guy who who'd been staring at the zipper asked.

Steve: I couldn't have picked a better name with a Bible. Steve rose and gave the guy who ignored the zipper a look. "Tell him I don't drink, Randy," he said.

"My step-father don't drink," Randy told everyone.

Steve stared down Randy. You could tell there was something between them, like respect. Steve sized up the kid and began flapping the 3 x 5 card. "Your mother's gonna read this," he told Randy.

"And do what?" the fatter woman asked, chewing spearmint leaf. "Spank his ass?"

"HOW CAN YOU TALK THAT WAY TO ME?" Steve said. He walked across the room, aimed his lip-smacking at the fatter woman. "HOW CAN YOU TALK THAT WAY IN THE PRESENCE OF A CHILD?"

The fatter woman grabbed his 3 x 5 card. The kid laughed. Steve's lips stopped smacking, his face stiff. He looked at Randy, then the hand the fatter woman had in her pants. "MY FIRST WIFE PASSED ON, YEARS AGO," he told her. "I MARRIED RANDY'S MOTHER IN GRIEVING. SHE SPENT MY LIFE'S SAVINGS, THEN THREW ME OUT OF HER BED IN THE NAME OF THE BAPTIST CHURCH. I SLEEP ON A COUCH IN THE BASEMENT, TO PLEASE GOD ABOVE. CAN'T YOU RESPECT THAT? CAN'T YOU FOR THE LOVE OF GOD RESPECT THAT?"

The fatter woman folded his 3 x 5 card.

"I'VE LIVED YOUR YEARS THREE TIMES OVER!" Steve told her. He reached for his 3 x 5 card and she slid it between the unbuttoned section of her blouse.

"And after all that living," she said, "you're gonna have to touch my sinful tits to get your card and your pretty little words."

Steve didn't do that. He crossed his arms and walked down the stairs, lips silent as the broken AM radio in my car.

■　■　■

Within half an hour, the guy who sold used car stereos sold a scratched JVC to me. Randy installed it, in his Baptist mother's garage. Then he led me back into his Baptist mother's living room. The ice in the cooler was floating. The kid sat on the three couch cushions watching the fat women snore. In the crystal bowl on the coffee table lay a single green ju-ju leaf.

"You don't guarantee it, do you?" I asked the guy who sold stereos.

He looked at Randy. He looked nothing like Randy. He looked tougher. "For a month," he said.

"How 'bout a receipt?" I asked.

"Receipts ain't worth the paper they're written on."

Randy looked at him, then me. His face looked soft—probably from too much Schlitz. "You got my number," he told me.

I patted my shirt pocket, my pants pockets, my ass: no 3 x 5 card.

"Here," a voice said.

It had spoken in melody. It belonged to the redheaded kid. His eyes were red, too. He was standing beside the coffee table, chewing the last spearmint leaf. He handed me a folded 3 x 5 card, which I put in my pocket. He wasn't a bad kid. The clear bowl was empty and the women weren't stirring. They were breathing. He's a good kid, I thought, and I have my 3 x 5 card and a new used car stereo. He's gonna be a good kid. He won't be a bad kid at all. Like Steve and me, someday he'll lose his fire to drink beer.

The kid, me and Steve, I thought. We're all going to be OK.

■ ■ ■

I woke up the next afternoon thinking it was May 27, but of course it was still May 26. Maybe I wasn't gonna be OK. Maybe June would take a year to round the corner.

I went straight from my bed to my Ford, started it, patched out down my street, flicked on my new used car stereo.

I did not hear a single Top Forty song. I heard static. I twisted the dials while steering and watching traffic. Then I was hardly watching traffic, so I pulled over. Then the static itself disappeared. I had nothing. I twisted the dials longer than an idiot would. I turned off the ignition. The temperature rose in my head. I stuck my head under the dash, to look at the wires.

There were at least three of them down there. Every damned one seemed OK.

■ ■ ■

I stayed up until 3:00 a.m., when I left for Randy's Baptist mother's used car stereo duplex. When I turned onto Bartlett, I saw RED, flashing red, so much red that nothing—not the street, the sidewalks, the trees, the houses behind the trees—escaped its stain.

A paramedic unit sat in the center of the red: on Randy's Baptist mother's narrow driveway. I pulled over four houses away, turned off my ignition and broken stereo, and got out. In the crown of a silver maple in Randy's Baptist mother's red front yard perched Steve. He was wearing the same robe, his blue slippers now gleaming purple.

"MY WIFE'S SON IS A DRUNKARD!" he shouted. "HE IS NOT MY SON! HE IS A PRODUCT OF MY WIFE'S FIRST MARRIAGE! WHAT AM I SUPPOSED TO DO?"

Two paramedics stood beside their unit, listening. One had a battery-powered megaphone.

"COME ON DOWN," the megaphone said.

"I WILL NOT COME DOWN! DO YOU WANT TO SEE WHAT THAT HEAVY-SET WOMAN SAID TO ME? DO YOU WANT TO SEE WHAT SHE SAID IN THE PRESENCE OF A CHILD?"

The paramedic with the megaphone looked at his partner, who shrugged.

"SURE," the megaphone said.

Steve paused for some serious lip-smacking. Neighbors were stepping onto their red front porches. Steve's arm pierced the maple's crown and dropped a 3 x 5 card, 3 inches by 5 of pinkened white cardstock that sailed, spun and flipped until it landed on the lawn like a mallard.

Red neighbors stepped onto red curbs. The paramedic without the megaphone walked across Steve's lawn and picked up the 3 x 5 card. Then he walked back to his unit, to see The Word better near the flashing red light.

He held the card in front of his face, held it closer, flipped it around. He handed it to his partner, who did roughly the same thing.

"WELL?" Steve yelled.

Neighbors were huddled in packs, packs of whispering red Americans.

"ALL I SEE HERE, STEVE," the megaphone said, "IS A PHONE NUM-
BER AND AN ADDRESS. *YOUR* ADDRESS, IF I'M NOT MISTAKEN."

That's *my* 3 x 5 card, I thought.

"What?" Steve said.

"THIS IS NOTHING BUT YOUR ADDRESS."

How did he wind up with it? I wondered. I thought hard about how he
did, then harder about telling the paramedics the whole story. I took one
step toward them when the one without the megaphone dashed toward
Steve's tree.

In minutes, he'd brought Steve down the earth. Steve followed him to
the paramedic unit, and a cold breeze crossed Bartlett, and Steve shivered
worse than the red silver maple leaves. I began toward the unit, but Steve
saw me and said "STOP." I did, out of respect. Then all that redness made
him appear frantic. Then he lay strapped to a wooden body board, head
erect, neck straining, probably thinking black rubber bag.

The paramedics slid him into the unit as men do themselves into the
women they love. The paramedics closed the unit, and Bartlett was as silent
as my stereo. May 27, I thought, and the unit sped off, taking the red with it,
leaving me standing in a circle of white streetlight.

My fingers inched into my pockets, feeling what I feared was still
there. I pulled it out and unfolded it. It asked me, in penmanship innocent as
youth but bold as shouting:

AIN'T YOU GETTING ENOUGH FUCKIN?

My lips smiled. My head shook itself No. I stood re-reading Steve's
card, spotlighted by white city streetlight, Randy and a fat woman who
expected love from the world no doubt looking on.

"Randy, there's the dude who bought the car stereo."

"Hey, stranger. Wanna stop by for a cold one?"

I kept smiling and reading. My head wouldn't stop. It kept shaking No
softly and I wasn't sure why: maybe for me, maybe for Kate, maybe for the

damned Bay Area and my damned used car stereo, maybe for that old Communist aura Capitalists are still trying to sell, maybe for what made Randy soft and that fat woman fatter, or for each Bartlett neighbor who'd returned to bed, all voting by silence to lie still and sleep—to turn 3 x 5 Steve into yesterday.

Undiscovered

*V*ic and Ray grew up learning licks in the same garages in Toledo, until they realized that two lead guitarists need at least two bands, when they moved, Vic to Detroit, Ray to Chicago. In the years that followed—separately—they did hundreds of two-bit gigs, grew their hair until it frizzed, tried drugs without names, slept with tattooed women, watched their fans marry and divorce, began their own bands, shaved their heads, fought with their drummers, and ate a lot of cheese sandwiches.

Now Vic, in the middle of his cross-country train trip, sat on a Salvation Army couch in Ray's loft in Chicago, flipping through Ray's pornographic magazines. That's the thing about undiscovered musicians, he thought as he studied a breast. They're always behind on rent, bitching about health insurance and bumming rides from people with cars, but they have plenty of food in their refrigerators, wine in their cupboards and interesting reading material. It's a good life, he thought. Why did I quit to teach high school?

"Hungry?" Ray yelled. He was washing his hair in the sink.

"No," Vic shouted.

Ray turned off the faucet and began wringing his hair. He didn't have much, but what he did have was long. "Someday," he said, "I'll have a pad with a shower."

"Sure," Vic said. "And someday we'll both be famous."

"Screw fame. Fame only matters until it becomes a nuisance. I want money, for Christ sake."

I want to be normal, Vic thought.

"Money," Ray said, "is power."

"I thought music was power."

"It is—to an extent. Music is energy. And energy gets women. Then women sap energy, and you need money to be able take two weeks off and do nothing but sleep, eat and make love, which is ultimately what you and a good woman want. I'm telling you, Vic, the nerds who went corporate were right: when it's all said and done, it comes down to capital."

That's why I teach, Vic thought. Though I still feel poor. And abnormal. I still stare out windows for no reason. "But those guys are miserable," he said.

"Maybe so," Ray said. "But at least I've finally set my priorities." He began drying his hair with a rumpled red T-shirt.

"Yet you continue to be Joe Rock-and-Roll."

"With one difference," Ray said. He tossed the T-shirt, dug a cigarette from between couch cushions, and lit up. "I'm going with simple lyrics. You know, score out a sharp baseline that'll lead to your solo, and don't make 'em think. Give 'em one phrase and keep repeating it."

"Such as?"

Ray squinted as he inhaled. "Jam It Good."

"That's going to bring you big dough?"

"You should see them dance to this number, man. And not just the girls. I don't want to jinx myself, but I might be one phone call away from Top Forty-ville."

"That and a woman who doesn't bitch all the time," Vic said, "and you're set."

Ray snubbed his cigarette against a withered pickle on a styrofoam plate. He stepped to the fish tank and fed his fish. "Something to eat?" he asked Vic. "I made this funky casserole the other day."

"How do you do casserole on a hot plate?"

"*Foil,* my friend. And your ingredients: one box of elbow macaroni—three for a dollar—a can of pork and beans—four for a dollar—and a handful of frozen peas. Some ketchup for taste, and you've got hearty eats for less than seventy-five cents."

He's beyond the edge, Vic thought.

"And what's great is, it tastes kind of mellow, so you don't eat much in one shot. I've been eating my last potful for six days."

Vic watched a black mollie rise and dart down. Ray and Vic cleared their throats.

"How old are we, Ray?"

An angel fish swam upside-down. Then he was fine.

"Forty-one."

"I think I'm forty-two. I had a birthday a few weeks ago."

"Shit," Ray said. "That's old."

"You'll be there next month, right?"

"Yeah, and I don't like it."

"You'll be fine. Look at Mick Jagger."

"I'd be better if I had Mick's money."

"If you had Mick's money, you'd be dead."

Ray walked to his yellow refrigerator, opened it and removed a pot covered with foil. He brought back the pot and two forks, sat beside Vic, gave Vic a fork, set the pot between them. Vic removed the foil and he and Ray ate, friends, as the fishtank hummed.

This has no taste, Vic thought. "What're you doing for women?" he asked.

"I've retired from groupies. That scene these days is nothing but, 'Can you get me on MTV?' I've moved on to the veterans. Especially tall and divorced."

Vic stabbed a tiny elbow.

"And yourself?" Ray asked.

"Not a kiss since I played my last gig."

Chewing, Ray walked to the door and opened it. A Saint Bernard bounded in, stuck its snout into the pot, then began sniffing its way toward Vic's crotch. "Shit, Christopher," Ray said. "Where'd you get this?"

I should do laundry, Vic thought.

"Check this out, man," Ray said, handing the pot to Vic.

Vic shoved the dog's snout toward the floor. Inside the pot was a dead bird, maybe a parrot. It was blue and yellow with a red patch on its throat.

"That's an illegal exotic bird, Vic. I swear the woman next door is smuggling and selling them. In fact, this proves it."

"How do you know it's from next door?"

"Christopher rarely roams far. Listen, I want to bust this woman. I swear she's smuggling these things, and I bet half of them die."

And I was beginning to like that casserole, Vic thought.

"You don't care, man? *Lives* are at stake."

"I care, Ray. I just don't know what to do."

"We gotta bust her. We gotta nail her."

"Well, where's your phone? I'll call the police."

"I already have. They say they can't arrest her unless they find the animals in her pad. And they can't search her pad without a warrant."

"And their excuse for the warrant?"

"They need someone who's seen the animals in there to sign an affidavit."

"Then why don't you sign one?"

"No more false affidavits for me, man. As it is, I'm sweating out that one with the IRS."

This, Vic thought, is what rock-and-roll leads to. Thank God I quit playing. I still have a shot at normalcy.

"So it's up to you, man," Ray said.

"To do what?"

"To go over there and eyewitness."

"Get outta here."

"Come on, man. Have you turned into an *absolute* sell-out?"

■ ■ ■

Vic knocked twice, opened the door and peeked in. An iguana sat on a large piece of driftwood, throat bulging, a rat's tail hanging from its mouth. On a purple hassock in front of a green curtain sat an old sewing machine, a Singer. A woman appeared from behind the curtain holding a gold tutu in front her face. She sat on the floor in front of the Singer—faced away from Vic—and began sewing the tutu. She wore a black oversized T-shirt and no pants or shoes and worked the sewing machine pedal with her hand.

"If you want to see me in this," she said, "ask."

A mirror hung on the far wall, the woman's reflection staring down Vic.

"I'm not here to see you," he said. "I'm here because my friend found a dead bird."

The woman snipped gold thread with a scissors and held the tutu in front of her face. "And I'm the prime suspect because my husband travels and I own a Columbian iguana." She tied the thread into a gold knot, stood, walked toward the mirror and pulled off her T-shirt. She appeared absolutely naked until she stepped into the tutu and Vic noticed her flesh-tone thong. She pulled on the tutu, worked its straps over her shoulders. I could've seen breasts in that mirror, Vic thought, if I hadn't been watching that thong. "What's your name?" the woman asked.

"Vic."

"Can you zip me, Vic?"

"Can't your husband?"

"He's sleeping on the loft. Come on. Zip me so I can see what needs doing."

Vic glanced at the loft. Lacquered-black magician's boxes sat there. The rat's tail gone, the iguana's tongue flicked like a horizontal yo-yo. Vic walked toward the woman and, erect, pinched the zipper. "Your husband's really up there?"

"He might have made himself disappear. He's a magician."

Vic was still pinching the zipper. "Your husband's an actual magician."

59

"Yes."

"If you're married, why no ring?"

"Rings don't make marriages."

"They help. At least that's what my girlfriend used to say."

"You have a girlfriend?"

"Had."

"'Had' because you were too into your career?"

"Exactly."

"That's how you see it. The truth is, you didn't have the balls."

"The truth is, you're not married."

"Try me."

Vic unzipped and pulled down his pants.

"Maybe you did have the balls." The woman pulled the tutu down to her waist. Her breasts, in the mirror, were small but upturned. Vic lifted her reddish hair off her ear, moved his lips toward her neck—and someone pounded on the door. Ray, Vic thought. "It's Johnny," the woman said. In the mirror, her eyes met Vic's. He let go of her hair. She walked to the door as he yanked up and zipped his pants.

"Mercy," a voice outside shouted, and the woman—Mercy?—opened the door for a round sunburned man wearing a ribbed white tank top and gray Dickies pants. The man walked toward Vic and extended his hand. "Johnny," he said. "My friends call me Johnny The Trashman."

"Hey, Johnny," Vic said as they shook. "The Trashman."

Johnny stepped toward Mercy's sink, poured a glass of water and drank loudly. The apartment began smelling like old lawn clippings. Mercy said, "Johnny's an actual trashman."

"Is that right?" Vic said.

Johnny nodded and worked down a last gulp. "Were you two about to jam?"

Jam It Good, Vic thought. "Of course not," Mercy said.

"Then why don't you introduce this guy?"

"Because," Mercy said, "I don't know his name."

"It's still Vic," Vic said.

Johnny nodded slowly three times. "Whatcha do to pay rent, Vic?"

"Teach music. Though sometimes I think I should quit."

"Let me give you some advice, Vic," Johnny said. "What you don't throw away can't hurt you."

I've thrown away rock-and-roll, Vic thought.

"Your refuse can hurt you," Johnny said. "Refuse hurt Nixon. Refuse hurt Dahmer. Leave something behind, it'll haunt you."

"Johnny's philosophical," Mercy said.

Johnny sat on a lacquered-black box beside the iguana. Vic's erection was gone. I hate silence, he thought. Maybe that's why I played the guitar.

"So what's the thought for today?" Mercy asked Johnny.

"You're not ready for it," Johnny said. "No one is."

"Try me," Mercy said.

"Okay." Johnny watched the iguana watch Mercy. "The Internet sucks."

"It does not," Mercy said.

"I told you you weren't ready."

"I'm ready for anything. You're just wrong."

"Let me put it as simply as possible. The potential for propaganda is unfathomable. Plus the Internet won't connect humanity like they say it will. It'll just distance the rich from the poor."

Engaging Vic's eyes, Mercy pointed at Johnny and rolled hers.

"You like the Internet because E-mail's a fad," Johnny told her.

"It is not," Mercy said.

"That's all it is. Plus it costs us."

"I use the Internet for free at work," Mercy said.

"Which means your office is paying for it. Which means they're expensing it against profits. Which means less tax revenue for government, which means fewer public services."

"Such as garbage removal," Mercy told Vic. "Which means Johnny might lose his job. Which is the real reason he hates the Net."

"The *Net*," Johnny said. "Let me ask you something, Merce. Who's pulling the profits off that thing?"

"I don't know."

I don't care, Vic thought.

"Rich conservatives," Johnny said. "Not the cool, young people you see on their commercials."

Maybe I do care, Vic thought. Conservatives hate rock-and-roll. What if they muzzle it?

"Rich conservatives fear communication with new content—because it threatens their power. But they love their money, so they continue to profit by changing communication's *form*. From hi-fi to stereo; from five-and-a-quarter-inch to three-and-a-half. The information is always the same: depressing. We just feel better when we own the new form."

Top Forty content has less taste than that casserole, Vic thought. Rock-and-roll will be trapped by the Internet.

"From albums to eight tracks to cassettes to CD's," Johnny said. "Remember when they had the balls to try quad?"

I oughta have balls, Vic thought. I oughta start playing again.

"I think CD's are great," Mercy said.

"Because they're a fad," Johnny said. "Which means you'll re-buy the music when 'compact' is supposedly too big."

"You're just old-fashioned," Mercy told him. "It's almost laughable."

"No one laughs at me when they remember I hated disco."

Mercy smiled sourly. Then her face sobered. "Johnny, you're sexually frustrated."

I'm sexually frustrated, Vic thought. Or maybe just frustrated period. Sex isn't my issue. My issue is music. Rock-and-roll will haunt me whether I teach it or play it. I'm gonna start playing again.

"Well," Johnny said. "My route calls."

But playing again seriously, Vic thought, would mean quitting teaching. And throwing away teaching might hurt me.

Johnny stood, cracked his neck and walked to the door.

"Next time you take out your refuse," he told Vic, "remember one thing: What you put on the bottom comes out on top." He stepped outside and the door closed.

The iguana watched Mercy watch Vic. She's waiting for me, Vic thought. We're all waiting for something. He walked to the sink, poured himself a glass of water, and, sipping, remembered his favorite part of his train ride to Chicago. He'd been sitting in the stalled coach car for over an hour, hating his stillness, staring out the window at trees, thinking a breeze was moving their leaves—until he realized that what was moving was the train. Which means *I'm* moving, he'd thought as the train rolled faster. He'd felt alive then, and the train began rocking. It kept rolling and rocking and rolling.

Pushing Ahead

I finally got a job managing retail. I know I should use the word woman. Sometimes I use the word girl. But see that's what people called them in college. This college I went to was Catholic. Enrollment was twenty-five hundred. Most of us hated going but had parents who expressed love with tuition. Education was an investment, they told us. So we paid them their love back by going. Lots of Iranians wanted to go to this college but couldn't. Iranians could only go if they made big donations and studied Christ for six credits. This one Iranian donated $600,000 out of his own personal savings. His name was Amad Al Ghatit. He put off studying Christ for three years but the college still named my dorm Al Ghatit Hall. So I lived in 6F Al Ghatit. I'd spell Al Ghatit whenever I called Dominos. But what was good was that everyone's room got refurnished. We all got these new modern phones. You could push certain numbers to make the phone ring in someone else's room. Today they call it call-forwarding but back then we called it pushing ahead. Girls with boyfriends back home pushed ahead to basketball players' rooms when they were sleazing around there. All the girls with boyfriends back home sleazed with basketball players. These were the thin girls without acne. These were the girls who told everyone else they were virgins. So when the boyfriend back home called in the middle of the night, the basketball player's phone rang. Of course the girl always answered. If it was for the basketball player she'd hand him the phone. Who cared if a girl answered a basketball player's phone? If it was the boyfriend back home the girl would talk on her boyfriend's dime from the basketball player's bed. She'd laugh while she talked, like nothing was happening. But stuff would be happening. The basketball player could be licking her clit-switch. Or maybe right in there scrogging. Either way the girl kept the mouthpiece near her face. Some girls would talk baby talk to the boyfriend and wink at the basketball player. Some girls were too busy to wink. It depended. It depended— the team thought that was funny. I know what they thought because I was senior equipment manager. I'd hand out their towels after games. At least two girls let basketball players fuck their asses. This was when ass-fucking was worse than donging your sister. This was before the gays were chic to have at dorm parties and got everyone thinking to fuck ass. When the gays were chic at dorm parties, everyone in Al Ghatit Hall fucked ass. Everyone laughed at those jeans commercials that never showed faces. Then Cyndi Lauper got hot and sorority girls started giving each other back rubs and fucking each others' fists. Then the law students started group-fucking in apartment complex jacuzzis. This janitor I knew mopped up the jag. Then some guy really did dong his sister. They actually dated for three weeks. Then the girls with boyfriends started fucking black basketball players. A lot of white basketball players didn't like this. See to be cool they were supposed to act like black basketball players weren't at all different from them. But it was also cool for white girls to fuck black basketball players so they could experience the difference. Guys who were racist didn't understand these kind of girls. These racist-guys grew up on ranches, so I guess you could call them cowboys. See this college was in Texas. If I said the name, that Al Ghatit guy would sue me. This one cowboy had a girlfriend with pencil point tits and blue-lensed glasses. He chewed a tin of Skoal a day and they'd fuck all the time. "Like monkeys" was the expression then. Every Friday after my Management class they'd empty the candy machines with two rolls of quarters. Then they'd lock his dorm room door and scrog all weekend with the lights on. Guys on our floor would listen under the door. This one biology major tried spying with a dental mirror. For a second one morning he saw the girl's knees. After the girl stopped her squeaky breathing everyone would stack lounge room furniture in front of the door. One weekend the stack didn't come down until Andy Rooney on *Sixty Minutes.* This same cowboy drove a pickup. His girlfriend liked fucking there also. One warm night she and the cowboy did the dog right in the truck bed. The guy with the dental mirror saw. He listened to Genesis and waited at his window for three hours. The girl kept her bra on but still. She also smoked Virginia Slims and the next day there were butts and tobacco juice puddles all over the parking lot. She was two years older than the cowboy. The cowboy was no genius. He took cake Psych pass-fail and flunked. His other grades weren't much better. But his dad had this ranch bigger than Delaware. So he'd end up ahead even flunking. This girlfriend of his liked nice clothes. He'd buy her silk skirts and panties and fuck her while she wore them. If they weren't torn he'd pay for the dry cleaning. But like most thin healthy girls she soon wanted to fuck black basketball players. Only there were no really rich black basketball players. The black basketball players got alum cash but blew it on gold jewelry and coke faster than wind puts out matches. So they weren't always rich. They weren't like ranch-rich. Now see this cowboy's girlfriend didn't snort coke. But she wanted to fuck black basketball players. But above all she liked her nice clothes. So on week nights she'd sneak over to the athletes' dorm and strip-tease the black basketball players in clothes the cowboy bought her. The black basketball players would put coke in her panties and snort it out with straws from McDonald's. She'd be straight the whole time. Then she'd do the push-ahead trick on the cowboy and fuck whichever black basketball player she still hadn't. Of course she was on the pill. All the smart healthy girls were. She took hers at lunch with Hi-C in the cafeteria. She didn't care when this priest who taught economics saw. And she didn't care if the cowboy was on campus when she did the strip thing. She didn't have to. On week nights the cowboy drank shitloads of Bud and passed out by midnight with Skoal in his cheek and his eyes open. Plus he was plain cowboy lazy. He'd never get up to pound on a door. The black basketball players knew that. The girl knew that. The cowboy himself knew it. He just didn't know the difference. During the day the cowboy laughed and high-fived with the black basketball players. He didn't use the N-word like other cowboys did. He wasn't racist. He snorted coke only once and flunked out of school in five years. After the girl quit smoking he married her. Black basketball players he laughed with do some of the work on his ranch now. One almost made the NBA. The girl doesn't work at all. The girl goes to malls and buys clothes. Sometimes she buys socks for her sons. My Lady's Wear clerks call her Master Charge Girl. I'm thinking of holding a meeting. They really should use the word woman. But then too they're all still in high school. They can still learn the difference in college.

Night Vision

Y ou've seen the ads. MAKE MONEY STUFFING ENVELOPES. Your initial thought was probably: Not worth pursuing. I thought that, too—initially.

If you want to pay rent, the hours get so long you need cola. One night, in such need, I dashed into the A & P a minute before closing. The cola aisle shelves were empty—except for a bottle spattered with mud. *Mine,* I thought as I grabbed. I ran to the counter, where a guy was purchasing bottled cranberry juice, frozen peas, deodorant and a can of chicken broth while flirting with the lovely Hispanic cashier. Her scanner charged him $9.79 for the chicken broth. I didn't mention it: I needed to get back to my envelopes.

The cashier raised an eyebrow, bagged his frozen peas. She had tiny black hairs on her arms, the faintest crow's feet, green eyes and a smile that actually sparkled. I looked again: a rhinestone appeared to be imbedded into her upper left incisor.

The flirt took his bag and left. I set down my cola and wondered if I'd imagined the rhinestone. Maybe envelope-stuffing had gotten to me. "Excuse me, ma'am," I said without flirting. "Is that a rhinestone in your tooth?"

"No," she said. "A diamond." She pulled back her lips as if preparing to brush her teeth. There it was, sparkling. "See?" she managed to say.

"That's quite something," I said. "How do you go about getting something like that … installed?"

"Superglued it. It used to be on my engagement ring. Before my fiance cheated on me."

"I'm sorry."

"Don't be. He could never finish anything he started. When I was near him I always felt lost."

"I had a girlfriend like that for five years once. Sometimes I think I'm still lost. The other morning I looked in the mirror and thought, Will that other me ever come back?"

The scanner beeped. "I know what you mean." I handed her envelope-stuffing income, which she studied as if it were counterfeit. "You know, we closed ten seconds ago. Would you mind walking me to my apartment on Tenth Avenue?"

"No. I mean, I wouldn't."

She bagged my cola and I took it. "Wait outside the doors for me," she said. "My manager hates when we're friendly with customers."

■　■　■

I stood on blue rock salt and frozen snow, losing envelope-stuffing cash by the second. She won't show, I thought. Probably left through the loading dock with the manager. And—dammit—she didn't give me my change. Then the door opened and she walked out beside a thin, graying guy pinching a lit cigarette. He gave me the skunk-eye, puffed, turned uptown and walked off.

"Hang on," the cashier said, watching him. Her manager, I thought. She handed me eleven cents. "Sorry," she said. "I guess I forgot."

She took hold of my left triceps and we began down Ninth Avenue.

"This is nice of you," she said, eyes on her feet. "I'm Karen. You seem like a nice person."

"I try. My name's Bob."

"You have an honest face, Bob."

"That I was born with."

"I like that—that I was born with."

We walked past the parked-and-Clubbed cars.

"What do you do, Bob?"

Tell her, I thought. If she wants a sugar daddy, she'll find out eventually. I cleared my throat. "I stuff envelopes, Karen."

"That's amazing: I just read an ad about that."

"It's honest money."

"Honest money." Karen squeezed my triceps. "I like that."

■   ■   ■

"I wish I had someone to watch TV with," she said on her stoop. Her diamond glinted streetlight perfectly.

"You mean tonight?"

"Well. Yeah."

"I could see watching TV."

"What about your envelopes?"

"That's the good thing about envelope-stuffing. You're your own manager."

"Tell me about it," Karen said, unlocking her door. She opened it; warmth pressed against us; she coughed and turned on a light. There was her TV, on her dresser. There was her bed, under a white comforter. "Studio City," she said. "That's my new term for Manhattan."

I followed her in and closed the door. She threw the deadbolt, turned on the eleven o'clock news, sat on the comforter, patted it. I sat where she'd patted and we faced each other. To avoid her eyes, I studied the diamond. Superglue, I thought. Then it was over: all of the love, hatred, cheating, and trust in the city had compressed itself into the twelve inches between our eyes.

"You think I do this all the time," she said.

"No," I said, and I meant it. Wow, I thought. From needing cola to ditching a manager to the precipice. And I like her.

So I kissed her. Her lips opened slowly. Her tongue flicked. Then my tongue flicked, nicking the diamond. We adjusted our torsos. Two of our hands—one from each of us—struggled to interlock. The fingers clasped and squeezed. Our tongues were still working. I felt strange saliva. Easy, I thought. I pulled back and cursed myself silently for not carrying protection; Karen rose and stepped to her dresser. She took off her coat, the A & P blouse, her jeans. Her satin blue panties clung. If the President were on TV declaring war, I'd read about it in the morning.

"I'm sorry," Karen said. She opened her dresser. "But I have this rule."

"Don't we all," I said.

"Yes, we do. I guess it's only a question of whether we follow it."

"I say we do."

"Good. Could you get the lights? Following it works better for me in the dark."

I stepped to the switch, saw Trojan-sky-blue in her hand, hit the switch, groped my way to the bed, sat on the edge of the mattress—and it descended again from her tininess.

We reached for each other. In the dark, she seemed older. Her panties were still on—until I stood and took off my clothes. Then we lay beside each other, cool and quiet, two aging children facing a wide slate of stars after skinny-dipping in a public pool. I played with the hair on her head. I kissed her neck. "No need to do that," she said. "I'm ready."

"Sheesh," I said. "You're fast."

"That's what my fiance used to say."

"Sheesh?"

"No. That I was fast."

"Did you want to talk about him?"

"No. I shouldn't have mentioned him in the first place."

"Then I guess," I said, "it's my turn to get ready."

"Yes, it is, Mr. Envelope Stuffer."

"Where's the … little rain slicker?"

"You don't have it?"

"I thought that's what you got from your dresser."

"It was. I set it beside you as we sat down. I thought you took it."

"I didn't see anything then. I have the worst night vision in the universe."

"It's right ... it *was* right here. And—shit—it was my last one."

I sat up. I began to decipher outlines of shapes. Karen was on her hands and knees, running her fingertips over the comforter as if giving a large massage.

"It was right here," she said.

"It couldn't have gone far."

"It's not here. It's gone. I'm not kidding, either."

"Then it's time," I said, "for my father's three rules for finding lost objects. The first one is—"

"Pray to Saint Anthony?"

"No. But we could have four rules."

"I'm sorry. I'm interrupting your father. Go ahead. Tell me his rules."

Now I was on my hands and knees, beside Karen. "Rules can be helpful," I said.

She sat on the edge of the comforter. "And I want to hear these. Seriously."

Seriously? I thought. "The first one," I said, "is 'Illuminate your area.'"

"Illuminating my area ruins the mood."

"As does losing the condom."

Karen remained silent. She was faced away from me. I pictured her lips pressed tightly against her Superglued diamond, possibly feeling pain. Watch what you say, I thought. She accepts you as a poor, honest envelope-stuffer.

"I thought *wearing* the condom ruined the mood," she said.

"That was five years ago. Those commercials affect a guy's mind after awhile. I mean, after all those commercials, I honestly get more excited when I roll one of those suckers on."

The mattress rose slightly. The light went on. There was Karen, small and naked, re-creating my mood in increments tiny as the hairs on her arm.

"What's two?" she asked.

"'Look *beneath* things.'"

"Then get off your thing—so we can look there."

I stood. We glanced at the condomless comforter, then shared one of those understanding expressions used by spouses of demanding marriages.

Karen looked beneath the bed, then beneath each of her three pillows. "If you think about it," I said. "This is kind of like 'Who Stole the Kishka.'"

"I don't know what that means."

"It's a song my grandmother sang. I think it has something to do with sausage casing."

Karen looked beneath her rug. "What's three?"

We sat side by side on the comforter. "Three." I cleared my throat. "Is 'Replace all despair with belief.'"

"That," Karen said, "won't be easy."

"And according my father, it's most crucial."

Karen hung her arm over my shoulder. "Well?" she said as we gazed at her deadbolt. "What do we do to start trying?"

Airstrip

G eoff bought an old Schwinn. He rode just before seven, after the eclipse of the 100-degree heat. His route took him past sheep pens, cattle pastures, tomato fields, vineyards. Ground squirrels crisscrossed the wheat-brown grass, and rabbits with shockingly large ears—jackrabbits?—sprang onto his path. If he didn't keep his mouth closed, gnats tickled the back of his throat. If he did, the smell of warm manure crammed his nostrils. After three miles of pedalling, he saw, behind a windbreak of olive trees on the right, an old asphalt airstrip with no tower or flagmen. Fifty yards later, on an intersecting path that dead-ended near the airstrip itself, he reached a horse he immediately named Brown.

Geoff turned and braked short of the horse's barbed wire pen. Brown, head drooped, wandered over. Fearing its thick teeth, Geoff petted it quickly above its eyes, feeling texture like the cowhide wallet his mother had sent him from Cozumel. Call her when you get home, he thought. She missed Dad enough before you left.

"I suppose you want carrots?" he asked Brown.

Brown's neck flesh twitched. A Cessna taxied down the old airstrip; Brown backed up and jigged.

"Try a DC-10," Geoff said. "From the inside. Into O'Hare."

■　■　■

The next evening, Geoff's mother's phone rang unanswered. Returning to the Poconos from Dad's grave, Geoff thought. Or trying a poetry reading at that café on Bleecker and 7th. Picturing her surprising calm nod of blessing the evening he'd announced he'd quit law ("After all," she then said, "that one partner *did* work for Nixon"), he replaced the receiver, then biked to the Safeway, where he bought four plume-topped carrots. Something about snapping each carrot in half helped him worry less about his mother, his father, his ex-girlfriend Charlotte—and the whole of Manhattan.

He scared six jackrabbits biking to Brown. A white horse, obviously male, faced the breeze in the center of Brown's pen. Brown, in the far corner, was tougher to sex. Geoff pulled half a carrot from his front shorts pocket. "Brown?"

Brown stayed. Geoff tried whistling, clicking, cooing—every nonsense sound he could imagine. The white horse walked over, snout aimed at Geoff's pocket. Across the path, a rusty sky blue pickup pulled into a half-circle of olive trees in front of a barn worthy of Wyeth. A man with a black lunchbox stepped out, looked squarely at Geoff, walked toward the open barn door. The horses are his? Geoff wondered—but the man hadn't spoken or gestured.

Geoff held the carrot-half over the wire. Now that another human was near, feeding Brown felt less important. The white horse stepped close, its lips passed over the carrot—and Geoff's fingers were empty. Its chewing sounded human, if louder, and then Geoff heard a bike braking and saw a gum rubber tire grab asphalt a scant four inches from his pedal. A woman wearing yellow-tinted sunglasses straddled the twelve speed's small black seat. "What're you feeding them?" she asked.

Geoff held out open hands. "Nothing."

The woman's hair was the color of old pennies, ponytailed and bundled with a large, violently twisted paper clip. Her legs, hips and waist looked as lean as a twenty-year-old's—*But this is California*, Geoff reminded himself, and her yellow lenses couldn't filter away the wrinkles beside her eyes. She glanced at Geoff's pocket: the carrot halves. A two-man plane touched down on the airstrip; the white horse trotted across the pen.

"Planes scare them," Geoff said.

"Can you blame them?"

The airstrip, Geoff realized, was as thin as the driveway behind his mother's new condo. "No," he said.

"You fly?" the woman asked.

"No."

"Bad experience?"

Geoff nodded.

"Same here. Follow me." The woman stood on her pedals, the back of her thighs ridged, trying to pump hard toward the airstrip. Geoff followed her, pedalling slowly, the front wheel of his Schwinn suddenly stricken with the ability to chirp. Beyond the dead end, the woman let her bike roll, her legs absorbing bumps in the sun-hardened sod. She braked on the airstrip. Geoff stopped at the edge.

"What's the matter?" she asked, straddling her bike.

"What are you doing?" Geoff said.

"Helping you get over it."

Near the far end of the strip, the tails of five parked planes formed a straight, silent line. A horse whinnied. The woman, crossing her arms, forced a smile. "Get out here."

Geoff dismounted his Schwinn and let it fall, then began a casual jog toward the airstrip.

"Bring the bike with you."

Geoff turned and backtracked, then considered not stopping, not even for the bike—just walking to his studio and driving cross-country to Charlotte's.

"I'm not going to kill you," the woman said.

Geoff pictured his mother setting fresh lilacs on his father's mica-flecked gravestone. He yanked up the Schwinn, swung a leg over the cross-bar; the woman grinned and pedalled toward the parked planes. A white broken line centered the strip and she snaked through the spaces. Geoff followed her slowly, keeping balance. She made a quick hairpin turn and headed back toward the end of the strip near the horse pen, her eyes, as she passed Geoff, avoiding his. He U-turned and followed her more closely, then was beside her, aimed at thick skid marks about forty feet from the end of the strip.

She squeezed her hand brakes, pointed at the black marks with her chin. "They touch down here," she said.

Geoff nodded and stopped, then heard the faint gargle of a plane engine overhead: at two o'clock high, a Cessna was taking a wide turn, aiming a descent at the strip.

The woman glanced at her black sports watch, pedalled beyond the skid marks, and stopped on grass the color of whisk brooms. Geoff rode beyond her—far enough that he felt safe from the oncoming plane—then looked over his shoulder. Still just off the edge, she was standing beside her bike, facing the plane, arms crossed.

"What are you doing?" Geoff shouted.

The plane droned. "Get over here," she said. "And let it fly over you."

"How's that gonna help?"

"You'll see."

Geoff turned, pedalled, and stopped three feet away from her, his bike, perpendicular to hers, aimed at Brown. He used his left leg as a kickstand, toed a pedal until it was high and ready. The plane, two thin lines joined by a growing dot, whined.

"Position your bike so you face it head-on," the woman said.

"Maybe next time." Geoff shivered. "I need an out."

"Typical."

Typical what? Geoff thought. The plane dropped quickly. For one moment he knew it was bound to land; for the next, that it might knock him flat. He didn't watch the approach—he listened. The engine's noise was surprisingly soft. After a wake of artificial breeze washed over him, he watched the plane's wheels touch asphalt. They didn't skid. They looked like toys.

"Did I see you trembling?" the woman said.

Was I? Geoff thought. "Not from the plane," he said.

The woman, arms still crossed, grabbed her biceps. "You sound like a student."

"I should."

"What are you studying?"

"English."

The word seemed to strike her face physically. "Here?" she asked. She scratched the back of her neck. "I mean, at the university?"

Geoff nodded.

"You criticize poems?" the woman asked.

"I imagine I will be."

The woman pedalled away. "Typical."

Geoff tried to catch up. "What's with this *typical?*" he asked—then realized he sounded more like his mother than he had when he'd lived in Manhattan.

"Typical man," the woman said. "In my experience." She was faster than Geoff over grass. She accelerated, creating distance.

"Tomorrow!" Geoff shouted impulsively, but she pedalled onward, headstrong. "By the horses!"

■ ■ ■

The next evening, Geoff fed the white horse a handful of Altoids peppermints. Again, Brown stood in the far corner. Within minutes, a coasting twelve-speed hissed: the woman, wearing an orange Body Glove T-shirt, the same tinted glasses tight against her face, her ponytail pulled harder. The old-penny-color of her hair looked cheap, but Geoff liked that. Did she ever, he wondered, mention her name?

She stopped five feet away from him, pulled off her glasses, wiped her brow with the back of her wrist. "So what did you want?"

Geoff thought he smelled Chapstick. "I haven't stopped trembling," he said.

She rolled her eyes.

"Actually," he said, "I thought we might bike together."

She pedalled away and Geoff followed. They passed Holsteins and vineyards, magpies and sheep studs. They coasted past white swan feathers floating on the muddy campus arboretum pond. When University Drive rose into view, she sped ahead and U-turned. Geoff followed her lead, pulled up beside her and copied her pedalling rhythm. They passed everything in reverse order; from the other side, it looked brighter. They didn't speak until she stopped at the horses.

"That was nice," she said.

Geoff bit a fingernail, dropped his hand to his side. "Does that mean you have to go?"

"What else would I do?"

The white horse kicked up fresh hay. In the half-circle of olive trees, the sky blue pickup sat empty. Geoff pointed at the airstrip. "I thought we'd stand under another plane," he said. "I'm still not over it."

Staring at his eyes, the woman blinked twice. Her hair hung in wisps over her ears.

"I'm not kidding," Geoff said.

She glanced at the horses, the hay barn, her watch. "It's late."

"Just one," Geoff said.

She studied the empty sky. "One."

They pedalled silently onto the airstrip and Geoff headed for their spot, on the grass just off the skidmark-stained end of the strip. The woman stopped on the edge of the strip itself.

"Today," she said as she dismounted, "the squeeze gets tighter."

Geoff pedalled a wobbly circle around her. "You're crazy."

"You want to get over it?" she asked.

■ ■ ■

At four the next afternoon, Geoff attended his first class, Feminist Critical Theory. According to the *Revised Schedule* it was a "seminar," but

Geoff preferred thinking of it as a class. Seminars, he'd thought when his mother had recommended the course the day before he'd driven West, were those issue-oriented meetings he ran while trying to make partner at the firm.

When Geoff walked into 230 Wellman, a stout, clean-shaven man of at least fifty stood in front of the empty desks. Geoff sat in the middle of the back row.

"Hello," the man said.

Sweat from Geoff's armpit striped his side. "Hi," he said.

"You're in the right room?"

"Feminist Critical Theory?" Geoff asked, and a woman, maybe forty years old, walked in. She sat in the front row and slid onto her desktop a five subject notebook marked PRIVATE. She ignored the clean-shaven man— who answered Geoff with a nod—and stared out the doorway as if someone in the hall were signing to her.

Another woman, maybe thirty, wearing what Charlotte used to call "corporate uniform"—short navy blue skirt, white gathered blouse, silver broach, black heels—walked in. She smiled at the clean-shaven man and sat to Geoff's left, near the windows. Then three women, between roughly thirty and fifty years old, walked in and sat in the middle of the room. They faced one another, whispering and frowning among themselves. None of them looked at Geoff. None of them looked at the clean-shaven man or the woman in the short blue skirt. The room grew warmer and a tall woman— easily six feet—strutted in and stood beside the clean-shaven man. She wore a purple scarf knotted against the left side of her neck; her hair was short, black, and capped with a comma of white; a mustard-colored gauze skirt— full-length—met itself between her legs.

"Ladies and gentlemen," the clean-shaven man said. "I'm Dr. Widener."

Geoff thought he heard someone hiss—but dismissed it as exhaust from an air-conditioning vent.

"And this," Widener continued, "is Ms. Morrill, a visiting instructor in the Philosophy Department. I was originally scheduled to teach this seminar, but after the protest last spring, the English Department has decided it would be best for all concerned if a woman—specifically speaking, Ms. Morrill—led your discussions."

No one moved or spoke. This *feels* like a seminar, Geoff thought. The woman in the front row stood and joined the women in the middle of the room.

"Very well, then," Dr. Widener said. "I hope you enjoy the semester." He turned to Ms. Morrill and extended his hand; they shook firmly and he walked out of the room.

"I think we should all get acquainted," Ms. Morrill said. She slid her hands into pockets in her skirt. "But before we do, let me take roll to make sure we're all where we belong."

The woman in the blue skirt coughed, crossed her legs and paged quickly through a *Revised Schedule.*

"Thank God he left," a woman in the middle of the room whispered loudly to another. "I can't stand the sight of him."

■　■　■

An hour after the seminar, which focussed on xeroxed excerpts by Adrienne Rich and Tillie Olsen, Geoff biked to the Safeway, then the horse pen. After the white horse ate six carob-coated pretzels, the woman on the twelve-speed arrived wearing pink shorts so tight Geoff felt guilty for noticing.

"This time we stand *between* the edge and the skid marks," she said.

"Why?"

"Because we must."

This time, they both watched the approach head-on. This time, the plane's tottering wings less than fifty feet overhead, Geoff shook.

■　■　■

Holding a golden delicious apple over the barbed wire the following evening, Geoff wondered if his mother, who, earlier that day, had—over the phone—told him his letters "smacked of sexism," might not be blooming into a feminist herself. The blue pickup pulled into the half-circle of olive trees; the farmhand walked into the barn without as much as a glance. Geoff stared at the gaping barn door until the sun was so low gnats glistened. At dusk he regretted his last decision in Manhattan—to throw his Seiko into the Hudson—then gave up on the woman and began biking to his studio.

In the middle of the arboretum, he saw her. She was coasting right at him and they almost collided while stopping. She chomped on cinnamon gum as she yanked off the tinted glasses. She fingered fresh sweat off her neck; strands of her ponytailed hair were sopped dark; she was breathing so hard through her nose Geoff wanted to tweak it.

"You're not going to the horse pen?" she asked.

"I was just there."

"Too early," she said.

"The sun was in the same place in the sky."

"The days are getting shorter, friend," she said. "That happens this time of year."

"Who said two people can't plan things by the position of the sun?"

The woman sighed and shook her head, a drop of sweat starring the asphalt. "We just can't."

"Why not?"

She frowned, set her hands on her hips. She's married, Geoff thought. Which explains her use of the word "typical." And the fact that she hasn't mentioned her name.

He felt himself blush and slapped his own face. "Sorry for asking," he said. "Maybe we should call it a night."

She slapped Geoff's other cheek softly, her hand hesitating, her finger-nails, cool, sliding against the grain of his stubble. "We'll meet on weekdays at nine," she said. She pedalled away, toward the horses. Geoff considered letting her go, then considered his alternative—reading the first half of *A*

Room of One's Own—and followed her. The sun was down when he rolled to a stop between his bike and the barbed wire.

"Still scared?" she asked.

"A little."

"You won't be," she said, "after tonight."

They rode side-by-side toward the strip. He stopped between the edge and the skid marks, where they'd stood the previous night. She let her bike roll onto the skid marks themselves.

"Let me guess," Geoff said. "Tonight we let a plane hit us."

She turned right and pedalled toward the far end of the strip, waving Geoff toward her. He followed, passing the parked planes and the orange mercury light on the side of the barn. She U-turned just off the asphalt and braked, her twelve-speed positioned as if set to race.

Geoff maneuvered his bike beside hers. Does she want to know *my* name? he thought. "I'll guess again," he said. "We're gonna watch it land down there and taxi toward us. That oughta be smashing."

"Don't get cocky," she said. She lifted her watch to her face. A plane's engine hummed from above, and suddenly everything was red: two strings of successively larger lights—the strip's night lights—lay glowing before them.

"Who did that?" Geoff asked.

The woman was reading her watch. "They go on by themselves." The airborne plane was taking the wide turn, its headlight focussed, it seemed, on Geoff's face. He felt like a circus act: if anything looked like a toy, it was him.

"Here we go," the woman said. She pedalled down the strip, toward the plane. Its headlight appeared to be too close, but Geoff, clenched by the panic of sudden trust, pushed off and followed.

"Tomorrow at nine," she said over her shoulder.

"Huh?"

"Pedal hard!" she yelled, and Geoff obeyed, aimed for the headlight. Wind clogged his ears and the woman crouched like a jockey, hair free of the paper clip, lips nearly kissing her handlebars. The headlight grew and

Geoff's legs pumped, the din of the wind giving way to the drone of the engine, the headlight dead-set for his locked arms, blinding him, sinking far too low—until cold wind rushed over his back. He curled off to the left, braked and looked over his shoulder. The plane taxied calmly. The woman was gone.

■　■　■

The next morning Geoff bought a cheap Casio, a six-pack of eggs, and—imagining his mother and Susan Sontag discussing his dating history over Earl Grey tea—a three-pack of laytex condoms. That evening, as he turned right toward the pen, the woman was petting Brown. She wore white bike shorts and a tight yellow T-shirt. Don't look at her that way, Geoff told himself. You'll end up as pathetic as Hemingway.

His bike squeaked as he pulled up behind hers. She turned and studied him, one eye squinting away sunshine, the fingers of her right hand tickling the underside of Brown's bulging jaw. "Ready?" she said.

Geoff nodded. The woman kept tickling Brown. She and Geoff didn't speak, just stood petting the horses. Knowing her name would ruin this, Geoff thought. Names and words ruin everything. Dusk filled in the crescent of olive trees across the path; the blue pickup still hadn't arrived.

When it was so dark the woman seemed faceless, she said, "Same end of the strip as last night." Her bike clicked, then hissed toward the strip. The strip itself, Geoff realized, was unlit. He pedalled toward it carefully. When he reached the far end, her bike lay on the edge, and she was pulling her T-shirt over her head, braless. He rushed a warm swallow, feeling shame. She pulled down her bike shorts—and the red lights flickered, then stayed on. Her shorts hit his front tire; she was clad in white French-cut panties. "I hope you're getting the idea," she said.

Geoff dropped his Schwinn and stripped down to his briefs. He faced the woman, stepped toward her. His fingertips touched the sides of her perspiring shoulders and squeezed—and she backed away.

Geoff couldn't think to say anything. He felt something closer to lust than to shame: the same feeling he'd felt when, as an attorney, he'd read *The Garden of Eden.*

"You think I'm that easy?" the woman asked. Her shoes were still on. Above and behind her, a two-man plane hummed.

"I was just trying to follow your lead."

She raised her glinting watch to her face; she stepped toward Geoff and grabbed his wrist. Warm French-cut cotton touched his thigh.

"We have to do something first," she said.

"You mean take precautions?"

She stepped back, yanked up her bike, lifted a leg over the seat. "I mean we have to … you know, on the bikes."

On the *bikes?* Geoff thought. The plane, twice as near, gargled. Geoff lifted his Schwinn, walked it toward her. His front tire nicked her pedal; his fingertips outlined her shoulder and neck—he kissed her.

"We have to ride first," she said. "Like yesterday."

"Why?"

She studied her watch, then pedalled to the edge of the strip. The two-man's headlight was making the turn, bearing down. "We have to get over it," she said.

"I'm as over it as I'll ever be."

She aimed her bike at the brightening headlight, toed a pedal. "I'm not."

"Let's go," Geoff said.

Her face didn't move. "We go when I say."

The white headlight vibrated, growing too fast.

"Now?" Geoff said.

"We've got to get over it."

"It's got to get over *us.*"

"It will."

It won't, Geoff thought. "I'm going only if you tell me your name."

"Now!" she yelled as she took off. Geoff froze, then pedalled, his front tire squeaking, thick wind pressing his chest. The headlight seemed to fall;

the engine backfired; the plane's wheels touched the far end of the strip and rose. Geoff ducked, braked and skidded, then spun off the strip, feeling the sting of scraped skin. The plane, behind him, flipped and slapped asphalt. Flames surrounding the cockpit shot skyward.

"Wimp!" the woman screamed. Her face, beyond the plane, reflected orange flame. "You're nothing but a God-forsaken wimp!" She was pointing, but not at Geoff; she was pointing at the cockpit and pedalling, beelining away. By the time Geoff crawled to his Schwinn and stood, she was gone.

Geoff was gone as well—halfway through the arboretum, racing back to his studio—when he heard the explosion. It had not, he realized, sounded as loud as he might have expected. Anyone else hearing it, he realized, might have figured it a prank pulled by boys.

■ ■ ■

Geoff lay on his bed naked, glazing the wound on his leg—it was the color and length of a fileted king salmon—with ice cubes, reading *A Room of One's Own*. After underlining "It is fatal to be a man or a woman pure and simple," he heard a thud on his only window. He listened to Wagner on the campus radio station—he could not concentrate enough even to read—then moved his curtain an inch to the right and peered out. Below the sill, on a holly bush, sat the first local paper he'd been delivered, rubberbanded and rolled diploma-tight.

He pulled on a pair of khaki shorts and walked outside. Snatching the paper as nonchalantly as pain allowed, he heard gears shift on a bike: a thin-shouldered girl, maybe nine years old, crossed the cracked asphalt basketball court across the street.

The crash, Geoff saw once back inside his studio, had made headlines. According to the copy, the pilot had died on impact. He'd been tenured at the University. His name had been John J. Widener.

"Please," Geoff whispered. He pictured Widener the only time they'd spoken: standing in front of 230 Wellman, hands clasped behind his back, pinheads of sweat on his smiling upper lip. The man had conducted himself so politely, Geoff thought. The man had, Geoff thought, appeared harmless.

He grabbed the crown of his head and continued reading.

Widener had published a few poems in his graduate school days but was better known for his criticism. For the past year, he'd been divorcing a "minor poet." The passenger of the plane, most likely a young female, possibly a student, was disfigured beyond identification.

"I'm not sure I'd use the word minor," Geoff told his undecorated wall. He dropped the paper and sat on the edge of his bed.

The phone rang. Geoff squeezed *A Room of One's Own.* Eyes fixed on the *V* in "Virginia" while the whole of him absorbed the ensuing expectant rings, he hoped Widener's wife had simply left town. He hoped he wouldn't be questioned; he hoped he'd be allowed to study feminist criticism as peacefully as a man could. Don't those of us guilty by association only, he wanted to ask whoever was calling, deserve that at the very least?

The Force of Pulchritude

*W*e decided to collaborate after my four novels hadn't sold and N. convinced me that, given the effect of feminist criticism on publishing, the only manuscript that could free us from the poverty my writing had forced upon us was a novel submitted under her name. To make this novel more marketable still, she suggested we make the narrator a Black female who'd been abused by an uncle. I knew Black dialect from playing basketball. N. knew abuse from her childhood. We'd never discussed that part of her past because she never brought it up, and I knew that, if I asked about it, she'd deny it. But I felt it—like a foot in a shoe feels a wrinkle in a sock. Because when I met her only uncle, he wouldn't look at me. And because she wrote the flashbacks about the narrator's abuse tearfully and quickly. The snag—in collaborating—occurred after the flashbacks, when the narrator's beauty was supposed to empower her: N. couldn't write about that.

So I took over. This was in the middle of western Massachusetts' worst-ever winter, snow banked so high we could barely leave our apartment beneath a bisexual chiropractor's office, and when we did, no matter how carefully I'd walk, I'd fall. So I stayed in and wrote the last sixteen chapters. Then line-edited the three N. had written so they sounded Black. When she saw the slew of my deletions and insertions, she screamed, wept and heaved at me whatever she could—including Sisyphus, our cat—because I was changing her *art*. I had to, I explained, so we could *live*. That wasn't the point, she said, and we argued and fought, and the fighting grew loud and physical. By physical I mean punching with me taking it. When I'd take it, I'd figure I was standing in for the uncle—or N.'s father, who'd left when N. was eleven, giving the uncle access—and the pain wasn't debilitating, so I took it. But then the sex went south. So I proofread the novel, visited the Suffolk Downs simulcast facility, hit a $321 trifecta, and used the cash to photocopy and mail to thirty-one agents thirty-one copies of the novel, *The Force of Pulchritude*, under N.'s name, her last name—Johnson—allowing racism to take its course.

And the agents jumped. They phoned, sent telegrams, drove up and rang our doorbell. One tried to peek through the blinds. Having anticipated this reaction given the *modus operandi* of agents who had wooed and failed me in the past, we'd changed the outgoing message on our answering machine to N.'s best impression of Nina Simone, then screened every call and never opened the door cold, responding to the agents' enthusiasm by mail only. All of which, of course, simply stoked their ardor until, a month later, we had our choice of publishing's finest, several of these offering their own advances on the prospective advances from publishing houses.

We signed with Louise Dimplethorpe, who'd Fed-Ex'd N. fifty grand. After N. banked the check, the fighting resumed, N.'s punches raising bruises on my forearms and shoulders, and then she began sleeping with a teenage neighbor who was confined to a wheelchair owing to an explosion at an Army Surplus store. So I needed to get out—of the relationship and Massachusetts—but all I had was thirty dollars, and I found myself in the bisexual chiropractor's office, telling him my troubles, and he offered me thirty-nine pair of velvet pants if I'd try each on in his presence, no touching involved. I could, he said, sell the pants for at least $200 apiece at any vintage store in Manhattan, so I did it—undressed and dressed thirty-nine times beside a massage table while he stood in a closet handing my pants. He remained stonefaced throughout and didn't touch me except a handshake as I left, and then, the pants in two cardboard cartons, I convinced N. to drive me to the bus depot in the Hyundai she'd bought with the advance, as well as spot me a ten so I could afford the one-way ticket. That's how I said good-bye—the words "one-way ticket." Her good-bye was a nod. As the bus began taking me from her, I looked out the window, and she looked back, her face blank, waiting, perhaps, for mine to spark something, but mine remained austere, and I wished I would cry—prove we'd had something to lose—but didn't, then considered waving, but what was the point?

So when I arrived at the Port Authority, I *had* to sell pants. And, I told myself, rent an apartment before sundown. Parting a flow of prostitutes and sailors, I stepped outside. Manhattan: What was the big deal? Yes, it was busy, but most cities were. The bisexual chiropractor had said the vintage stores were "around Eighth Street," so I taught myself the difference between Avenues and Streets, then headed downtown.

At 31st Street, the cartons were pinching a nerve. I set them down and watched part of Manhattan's throng approach and pass. Harmless. I hoisted the cartons, walked to 18th, sat on the cartons. Sunshine reached me from a gap between roofs. Then I walked on, resting every two blocks, until I made it to James' Vintage, where I set the cartons on a counter.

The place was nothing but tiers of hanging clothes except for a Black woman behind the burlap curtain in front of the fitting room. Given the contrived calm with which her turquoise eyes met mine, I'd caught her in a moment of nudity. Then, from a gap between the bomber jackets and the leather vests, limped a man eating a mango. Buzzed hair and black safety glasses over leaden eyes dull as death.

"Yes?"

"I have some pants to sell."

"And?"

"I'd like you to buy them."

"My pants are barely moving."

"These are velvet."

He opened a carton, took out a white pair, raised its waist over his head. Fingered a cuff, placed it into the carton, removed a mustard-yellow pair. "How many total?"

"Thirty-nine. They're Italian."

"I see that."

"They're virtually new."

"Which detracts from their value. I'll give you ten each."

Equals $390, I thought. The bisexual chiropractor, I remembered, had said studios with toilets in their kitchens went for $700.

"Some of these," I said, "cost fourteen hundred dollars."

"So?"

"I want two hundred apiece."

"Don't be absurd."

I snatched the yellow pair, tossed it into the carton, set both cartons on my head.

"Fifteen. But that's charity."

I turned and walked quickly. Outside, sparrows chirped. I had value, I knew, and this time—unlike with *The Force of Pulchritude*—I wouldn't blow it. I needed another vintage store, where I'd play hardball from the start. I walked on, passing warehouses. "Listen," I heard, and I turned and saw the woman with the turquoise eyes. Her pout and pensiveness exuded beauty, but beauty, right then, felt worthless—but then, from a pocket inside her pea coat, she removed a checkbook. "I'll give you a hundred a pair."

One-fifty, I thought, though I found myself saying, "As long as it's cash."

"Then we'll have to go to my apartment. On 43rd."

"Fine."

"You a cop?"

She's a whore, I thought. "No," I said, and we faced uptown and began strolling.

"What are you?"

"A writer."

"You don't look like a writer."

"For that I'm thankful."

She smiled and I thought: So she's a whore? When you're broke, a whore is like anyone. Then her palm displayed two translucent red orbs. I tried to ignore them, then felt tongue-tied.

"What are those?" I finally asked.

"Candy coins. Try one." She pressed a blur of redness past my lips, its surface brackish, its insides sweet. Chewing provided purpose to our sputtering conversation. She, too, was chewing. Our shadows, ahead of us, seemed to be pulling us.

"What's the big deal—" Because of the candy, my jaw felt wired. "About Manhattan?"

"I know what you mean. It's the country that's a bitch. You ever live in the country?"

"Unfortunately."

Then I told her about Massachusetts: slipping on the snow, taking the punches, modelling each pair of pants for the chiropractor in exchange for the pants themselves.

"So you're a whore," she said.

"No. He didn't touch me."

"But he got off watching you."

"No, he didn't."

"Sure, Baby."

"What does that mean?"

"He got off after you left."

"Well, I didn't enjoy *my* end of the deal."

"And you got paid to do it. That makes you a whore. So don't act so priestly around me."

The cartons grew heavy: I was slowing our pace. As if reading my mind, she took one, hugged it, and we walked on.

"You know when I was *really* a whore?" I said, and I told her about writing and selling *The Force of Pulchritude.*

"So your sugar," she said, "got the fifty."

"Yes."

"So you stripped for that guy for your fuck-you money."

"Uh-huh."

"Nothing personal, but it's good to see that kind of pinch happening to a man for a change."

We didn't speak but walked comfortably. I thought about N., her teenager, her agent. Pathetic, all of them, but I didn't feel sorry for the agent. I felt sorry for N. Fifty grand barely dents being diddled by one's uncle. And the teenager deserved pity. He couldn't walk *plus* he had N. Though he probably had a large negligence settlement from the Army Surplus store. N. and he were rich. Still, they'd be miserable.

We climbed four flights of stairs to the whore's place. It was a room, really. A bed, a nightstand, a lamp, a chair. Daffodils in a plastic-and-foil-wrapped shoe box on the sill of an open window.

"No fridge?"

"I eat out." She reached out the window, slid her fingers between the foil and shoe box, pulled out an azure Hallmark envelope, opened it and removed a wad. Counted bills and handed them over, opened the cartons and began counting pants.

I sat on the bed with the cash. On the nightstand was a stack of electric pink Xeroxed sheets. I glanced and read "RULE 5: NO CRUMBS." I counted the bills. Thirty-nine hundred. Now all I needed was a roof, which was supposed to be impossible in Manhattan, but I didn't believe that. Or maybe I didn't want to leave *there*. The simplicity of her room, the ease of our deal—I liked her.

"What'll you do with the pants?"

"I know dancers."

So she'll profit, I thought. "You're a dancer?"

"Used to be."

"Why not now?"

"I used to dance at this place that had this back room with these booths divided by windows with six-inch-wide holes—you know, the kind you can talk through?"

"Uh-huh."

"And this old guy, maybe seventy, would take me back there, pay me a Benjamin, drop his pants and tie dental floss around his balls. Then he'd shove the other end of the floss through the hole and have me hold it while I stripped and fingered myself, and when he'd finally get hard, I had to yank the floss and say 'Elton's a very bad boy.'"

"So?"

"It was belittling."

"Maybe he wanted belittling."

"It belittled *me*. He'd also take a match and light it and stick the bottom of it up his ... you know, peehole. And have me finger myself while it burned."

"He'd let it burn all the way down?"

"The flame would be a millimeter away and he'd come. And that match would *fly*. And he'd aim it at the hole. And rarely miss. And get mad if I ducked. It was awful."

"I imagine."

"Whoring at home is loads better."

"Not belittling?"

"Compared to dancing it's truffles and pudding." She grabbed my wrist, let it go. "Because I set the rules. No foreplay involving fire, no floss— I xeroxed a hand-out." She nodded at the pink sheets.

"I noticed. They're nice. But doesn't your ... pimp set the rules?"

"*Pimp*. This is the Nineties." She sat on the bed, less than a foot from me.

"You don't have one?"

"I did. I put my foot down. Which is what you should do with your girlfriend's agent."

"Ex-girlfriend."

"Whatever. You should tell that agent you want your cut. I mean, you wrote the novel, right?"

"Most of it."

"Then the proceeds are mostly yours."

"But they're in her account."

"That's an advance on an advance. Which means there's more coming."

"You think?"

Fretting, she nodded. "Slimy projects *always* pay off well in Hollywood. In fact, your book probably already has."

She's right, I thought. There's money out there and it's mine. And if I had it, I'd be set. No stripping for pants or standing in to take punches or posing as someone I wasn't.

"Let's go," the whore said. "Visit your agent."

"She won't give me money."

"You think so."

"I know so. I've dealt with agents before."

"So have I."

"Yeah, but as a dancer."

"Yes, but before that I was an editor."

I didn't believe her. The turquoise eyes were undoubtedly contacts. "Wait. You were an editor ... and *then* a dancer?"

"Yeah. See, I couldn't move up the ladder at those houses without using my tits. And the titles I worked on bored me to pieces. So I figured, why kid anyone? Anyway, think about it: Hollywood won't go for that book if word gets out it was written by a homeboy."

This woman, I thought, has great ken. And an apartment. And she's beautiful. "Okay," I said. "Let's go." Just don't begin feeling, I thought.

We left the room and she stepped to her neighbor's door and pounded on it. A Black man answered—eating an ice cream sandwich. "You're not my pimp anymore," she told him.

"Then I guess," he said, licking his fingers, "I'll be kicking your ass."

She pointed at me. "With Vice Squad around?"

The man studied my face. I was pissed at my whore-friend but glaring at him, so maybe I looked like a cop. Say something, I thought. Something

Joe Pesci. "Do what you have to," I managed, then stared him down as if I'd just tweaked his throat with a razor.

He grabbed his jaw and nodded, and my friend's elbow nudged mine, and she walked toward the stairs, and I followed. Run, I thought. "Walk slowly," she whispered. Was she right? She was smart. The pimp's door, from the sound of it, stayed open.

Outside, 43rd Street looked busier.

"I thought you didn't have a pimp."

"I don't."

"You did when you told me you didn't."

"No, I didn't. I had you. I just needed to give him the message."

"And you used me for that."

"Like you'll use me now. Where's that agent's office?"

"Twenty-fourth." This I remembered because the check for fifty grand had arrived the day before N.'s twenty-fourth birthday.

"Are we talking about Dimplethorpe?" she asked.

"Yeah." She *was* an editor, I thought.

"Then we have to go back." She grabbed my wrist to stop us.

"Why?"

She squeezed. "You have to change your pants. That mustard yellow velvet'll work perfectly on Dimplethorpe."

"What if your neighbor sees me?"

"Then he sees you."

"Won't the pants blow my cover?"

"You're *Vice,* Baby. You're always changing your look."

Now I was scared. She couldn't have known Dimplethorpe—not really. She was angling me, I was sure, toward something else she needed to have done.

"Listen," she said. "If this visit's going to work, I have to show Dimplethorpe an *author.* Which you'd pass for if you'd put on those slacks."

Landing a foot from us was a squat, white pigeon. "What if they don't fit?"

"I thought you tried them on in front of that chiropractor."

"They were tight."

She pulled her pea coat lapel enough away from her to expose a naked breast, a C-cup with a nipple the length and hue of half of a burnt sienna Crayola. Implants, I thought, and she cupped the base of her breast and squeezed, launching a wire of milk that tickled my eyelid.

I knuckled my eye clean. "So you're a mother," I said.

"Yes and no. I had a son, but I gave him up."

"Why?"

"I'm too into sex." We watched the pigeon peck grit. "And I can't control myself around money."

"So you'll want some of my take from Dimplethorpe."

"Ten per cent. Or twelve and you can live at my place for a month."

"Next to your pimp."

"Ex-pimp." She smiled—trying to pry me? "And you can fuck me whenever you want."

"Right. With your clients there."

"When they're there, you'll hide in the closet. Or go for coffee." She covered the breast, folded her arms over the coat. "And don't worry. I use condoms." The pigeon fluttered and flew off. "Well?"

"I don't think so."

"What if you have to?"

"Then I'll have to."

We walked back to her place eating her coins. On the stairs in her building, I saw that the pimp's door was open, the doorway empty. Inside her apartment, I changed into the mustard yellow pants, which felt tighter than they had when I'd modelled them. She opened the door: in the hallway, the pimp dragged two overstuffed pieces of luggage toward the stairs. He saw us and continued, and she walked out, and, again, I followed her past the pimp, who nodded and muttered, "I'm outta here."

Outside, I saw clouds. At 33rd, the velvet had loosened. On 24th, my whore-friend knew which building was Dimplethorpe's, as well as the name of the doorman, who told us the office itself was on six. I envisioned that long nipple as the elevator rose. Did her clients suckle her milk? Would the taste turn me on? Forget the nipple, I thought. Give her ten per cent and—at worst—find a hostel. Then I thought realistically: Ten per cent of *what?*

From the outside, Dimplethorpe's office looked like an apartment. We were buzzed into a living room, where we waited beside a vacant reception-ist's desk. Hard-covered volumes on gold fixtures graced the walls. Then, from what appeared to be a bedroom, strode a thin fellow in his early twen-ties. Dimplethorpe's lackey? Exuding the relaxed distinction of Harvard graduates, he told us his name, which I promptly forgot.

"Where's Louise?" my whore-friend said.

"Madagascar."

"And I'm in Prague. Tell her Shirley's here."

Non-plussed, the lackey folded his arms.

"And that I'd like to speak to her now."

"She's not here, Shirley—I'm sorry—I missed your last name?"

"Just Shirley. And after I leave, tell Louise to teach you who's who."

The lackey blushed, retreated to the apparent bedroom, and closed the door. Another five minutes of waiting. Then he returned with a monitor attached to a gray extension cord. Set the monitor on the desk, opened a drawer, removed a remote and an apparatus that looked like a cross between a blow-dryer and a large revolver. Aimed the remote at the monitor and punched it with his thumb—and the screen brightened into lavender clouds that evolved into a pale woman's face, eyes blinking, eyebrows pencilled, lips recast beyond their borders with glossy taupe, a pair of chained reading glasses damming graying copper curls. Shostakovich played softly from the sides of the monitor, then faded. The lackey pointed the apparatus, which was equipped with a lens, at Shirley's face. "Louise can see and hear you," he whispered.

Dimplethorpe's image quit blinking. Then it said, "I'm headed for a zebra safari. Speak clearly and get to the point."

"We'll take a hundred grand," Shirley told the apparatus, "if the safari need prevent us from negotiating."

"Negotiating what?" Dimplethorpe asked.

"The proceeds from …" Shirley faced me. "What was the title?"

"*The Force of Pulchritude*," I said, and the lackey aimed the apparatus at me.

"Who's that?" Dimplethorpe asked.

"The actual author," Shirley said. "And he has the rough drafts to prove it."

"Take a hike," Dimplethorpe said.

"We can do that," Shirley said. "To the *Times*. Where Chuck McGuire would be exceedingly pleased to hear our story."

Dimplethorpe's image froze, mouth snarled. The bedroom door opened and she emerged in the flesh. Less than five feet tall, she was eating salami on rye. "You're snowing me, Shirl. Leave or I'll call security."

"Call," Shirley said.

Dimplethorpe lowered her glasses over her eyes. She studied Shirley, my hair, my pants.

"Louise," I said. She wouldn't face me. Why not? I wasn't sure what to say next, but the moment seemed mine, and after tough-talking that pimp, this was nothing. "I know you've never seen Ms. Johnson. And that you sent someone to Massachusetts to see if she were Black. Which she isn't."

"In fact, no agent—or editor—has seen Ms. Johnson," Shirley said. "Because she and my client were hiding. Because *he* wrote that book. And now you want to sell it under the pretense that the author's an African female? Louise, those are facts *any* journalist would kill for."

The phone on the desk rang. Dimplethorpe glanced at it, faced me, and said, "Five thousand. But then this meeting never happened. If I hear rumors that it did, you won't publish a syllable in this town."

"Fifty," Shirley said.

"Nine," Dimplethorpe said.

"Fifteen. If we can cash the check today."

Dimplethorpe bit into her sandwich. Chewing, she stepped into the bedroom and returned with a blank Chase Manhattan check that depicted a rainbow and several balloons. She asked me the spelling of my name, which I told her, then sat on the desk and wrote the check for fifteen thousand, her expression appearing as numb as mine had felt when I'd left N. in Massachusetts that morning. She tore the check free, scissored it between fingers, and allowed me to take it. "In the long run," she told me, "I'm going to beat you."

"Which leaves the short run," I said, and I stepped toward Shirley, stood face-to-face with her, imagined waking up beside her, and kissed her. I kissed her long enough to make it clear I'd give her twelve per cent at least, then—hellbent if ever—led us out of there.

Trust

T odd slit the belly and orange eggs oozed: this keeper was female. He yanked out the heart and the tail slapped the sand. Alive, he thought, and he laid it on its side and struck its head with a wrench. The gill relaxed. Its skin was sandy, so he walked it to the end of the dock, dunked it—and it shuddered and swam off.

"Shit."

"What," Fitzie said.

"She swam off."

"They'll do that if you don't hold 'em right."

"She was *gutted.*"

Maybe, Todd thought, she'll swim back.

He watched the water. "That," he said, "was a smart fish."

"Or a dumb fisherman," Fitzie said, and the old-timers laughed.

"At least I get laid," Todd said, but they laughed on, as if sex didn't matter. It did matter, didn't it? Not to them—because they were old. But it didn't to Gwen, and she was 29. She's frigid, Todd thought. Though Arvy would disagree. She needed fresh stimuli, according to Arvy's *Fabulous Intercourse: Volume One,* and she would climax if Todd touched her in new ways.

Todd packed his tackle, got in his Dart, fastened the door to the headrest with the coat hanger wire, jammed the screwdriver into the ignition and cranked. The old-timers laughed harder. He cranked hard and the six-banger roared. "Sometimes I win," he yelled, and he revved it and they stared at their floats. They didn't care. Nobody did. He'd have to care. Then Gwen would be fine. He dropped it in drive and flew onto the smooth highway. He would be smooth with Gwen—showered, shaven, teeth and tongue brushed—and he'd ease into intercourse, kissing east and west rather than south. He'd try all of Arvy's suggestions, and she'd lose her mind and be fine.

He curved past the thoroughbred farm, then straightened out through town. Gwen's Gremlin wasn't beside The Chili Cafe: she was home. He glanced at his odometer—42—braked to 30. Easy, he thought. Everything slow, smooth and easy.

He turned into the lot and pulled up beside the Gremlin. The Dart died. He threw it in park, hid the screwdriver under the seat, got out and climbed the stairs and walked in. She wasn't in the kitchen. She was in the bedroom, naked, on the bed, on her stomach.

"My ass sags," she said.

Quote Arvy, Todd thought. "It's perfect. And so is the rest of you."

"What kind of bullshit is that?"

Todd took off his shirt, pants and steel-tips.

"Where's the keeper?"

"I, uh. Released it."

"That was our supper, Todd."

"We'll have something else."

"All we have is liver. Frozen."

"Gweneth." Todd sat on her black hassock. "Don't worry so much." He stretched his legs across the back of her knees.

"You been reading that book again?"

"Yes. And it says I should touch you in new ways."

Smoke hissed from the side of Gwen's mouth. "Maybe you should suck off my fingernail polish."

$24.95, Todd thought. And four days of reading.

"Books are scams, Todd. One idiot writes something and another idiot prints it, so all of sudden it contains wisdom?"

But Arvy's wife climaxes, Todd thought.

"I should write a book," Gwen said. "It can't be that hard."

"What would you say?"

"That men should put women on their hands and knees and fuck them like horses." She shoved Todd's legs off hers, propped herself on her forearms, pulled her knees beneath her, raised her ass.

Rear-entry won't satisfy, Todd thought. I *must* satisfy. "But what about you?"

Smoke rose past Gwen's perm. "What about me?"

"I want you to like it."

"I like getting fucked."

"I want you to climax."

"*Cli*max. Say 'come.' Anyway I want to enjoy this cig."

"Then I'll wait till you finish."

Gwen rotated her ass. Todd's cock thumped and thickened. No, he thought. Well, maybe. No: Wait and be loving. Okay, but after you go east and west. He took off his boxers. Kissed Gwen's freckled shoulder.

"Just get the K-Y."

Well, Todd thought. Chapter 4 said to do what they ask. He opened her lowest dresser drawer, reached under her sweaters and abandoned dildo. The K-Y felt steamrolled. "We're out."

Gwen licked her fingertips, reached behind her, slicked down the hairs. One might have been gray. Experienced, Todd thought. She needs someone experienced like Arvy. He knelt behind her, worked the head between the lips, tried an Arvy suggestion—extremely slow stabs—and she relaxed, stiffened, then re-lit her Marlboro. Began picking crumbs off the mattress. "Are these from your graham crackers?"

Fuck, Todd thought. "Yes." He coughed. "Sorry." He quickened it to get it over with, felt love and hatred and one or two squirts. It wasn't like when he was 20. He withdrew, coughed, reached for a Kleenex from the box beside her jeans, saw something in her pants, in her panties. It looked like a small flying saucer.

"Something wrong?" Gwen asked.

"What is that?"

Gwen twisted her Marlboro. "What."

"In your pants." It was round and the color of pale skin. Todd pinched it, held it near his eyes. "An oyster cracker."

Gwen yawned. Yawned again.

That cook, Todd thought. She's fucking that cook Ned to achieve climax.

Ned looked the way Arvy wrote: intelligent, tall, confident, charming. Everything Todd wasn't.

"So?" Gwen finally said.

"So what was it doing in your pants?"

"I guess it got in there at work."

"You guess?"

"I mean it must have. I didn't feel it, but it must have."

"You didn't feel a *cracker* in your pants?"

"If I had, I would've tossed it."

"How did it get in?"

"I don't know. Yes, I do. These kids were in today—guys on one side, girls on the other—and I served their waters and oyster crackers, and a girl threw an oyster cracker at a guy, and he threw one back, and the next thing I know they're all throwing oyster crackers. By the handful. I guess I got caught in the cross-fire."

Bull, Todd thought. And if kids had been throwing anything, he wished he'd been one of them: Youth offered hope in maturity. "How old were these kids?"

"Like twenty. You know, the college kids. They're back now, you know."

"But how did this get in your *pants?*"

"I don't know. I was wearing my relaxed-fits. I would've worn my hiphuggers but you said you didn't want me wearing those there."

Todd hung his head.

"Toddie, there were a *lot* of crackers. It was like standing in the middle of a blizzard."

Alright, Todd thought. Show balls. "Where was Ned during the blizzard?"

"In back."

Todd felt his mind freeze.

"Making chili."

"Why didn't you go back and help him?"

"Can't. The register's out front."

So lock it, Todd thought. "So?"

"If I'm short at shift-change, it comes out of my check. And those kids would steal. Even with all that money their parents send them. They're bastards, those kids. I hate them."

Another question, Todd thought, and you're back whacking off in Ed's rooming house. He pictured the sign in that bathroom: KEEP TOILET SEAT CLEAN OR RENT RISES.

"I hate them," Gwen said. "It was so nice this summer without them." She got out of bed. "And their books." She studied herself in the dresser-mirror, placed her palms over her breasts and squeezed. "I'm going to work."

"Already?"

"You're not mistrusting me again, are you?"

"No." Todd grabbed his jaw, let it go. "But there's two kinds of trust: one where you know everything's fine, and one where you don't but you gamble."

"Says who, Arvy?"

"No. Me."

In the mirror, Gwen caught Todd watching a squeeze. Her hands fell. "Which do you operate on?"

"With you?"

"Of course."

"A little of both."

"How little."

"Enough that I'm here."

"Listen. You catch me fucking Ned, I'll give you a thousand dollars."

"You don't have a thousand dollars."

"I'll get an advance from my VISA." Gwen held her red hair brush an inch from her forehead. "Or, if you prefer, submit to touching in new ways."

"Maybe you should submit so I *don't* catch you."

"Maybe, if you'd trust me, I'd come."

Trust? Todd thought. Arvy wrote nothing about trust.

"Who knows?" Gwen attacked her hair tangles with surprisingly hard strokes. "It's not working your way. And let's not talk about it. Talking about it makes me feel like I have to, and feeling like you have to doesn't help."

Forget it, Todd thought. Just fuck her, fish for your self-esteem, and keep an eye on that Ned.

"And to be honest, Todd. If you can't trust me, maybe we should …"

"What."

"Nothing."

"*What.*"

"Never mind."

"Break up?"

"I didn't say it."

"But that's what you meant." And you meant it, Todd thought, because you don't *come.*

Gwen yanked fresh jeans from her top dresser drawer. "I gotta go."

"Don't feel like you have to."

Scowling, she pulled on the jeans. "The money won't hurt." Hiphuggers, Todd noticed. "And seeing you let go that keeper …" She wiggled in and zipped. "I'll bring back two quarts of extra-hot."

Ned's extra-hot, Todd thought. And she's not wearing panties. "What could I do? The thing played dead."

"You could have held it right." Gwen stepped into the bathroom, grabbed the Lavoris, shut the door. "There's a way to hold a fish," she shouted, "so you don't lose it."

"Just bring home that chili," Todd told the door. "I'll be starved."

■ ■ ■

Todd squeezed the kitchen window frame as Gwen's Gremlin barrelled off. He wished he had work. He wished he had height. He remembered the day he answered a knock on Gwen's screen door and Ned, peering in, didn't see him.

That was bad, he thought.

Arvy claimed height didn't matter, but Arvy was probably hung. *That's* why his wife climaxed. The stuff about touching was bullshit. Guys with small pricks got enlargements or lost.

But I can't even afford wax worms, Todd thought. Unless I catch her and she pays me that grand. But why stay with her then? I'll catch her and leave. I'll get them on film to have proof.

He stepped to Gwen's junk drawer. Beneath her tabloids were snapshots from the day they'd played models to try for her climax. He studied a snapshot: pubic hair, his. Where was the camera? In her *trunk*. From the night they'd played nudists—and mosquitoes had bitten his ass.

■ ■ ■

Gold spinning lures hung, each over $3. Behind the counter, Jeff watched *Geraldo* on a small black-and-white.

"Hey, Jeff," Todd said.

Jeff didn't answer, but when Todd talked, that happened.

"You got a camera, right, Jeff?"

Jeff looked up.

Todd pointed to the lunker photos taped to hell against the counter. "The thing you take these with."

Jeff nodded at a Polaroid behind the turkey jerky. "But your keeper's long gone."

He means Gwen, Todd thought. "Says who?"

"Fitzie." Jeff faced the TV. "Said you don't know how to hold 'em."

"Just gimme the camera."

"Five bucks."

"No way."

"Fine. Buy your own."

For $50, Todd thought. He pulled out his wallet, thumbed his cash: four ones. Dug in his pockets: a nickel, seven pennies, one used split-shot sinker.

"I don't want that crap."

"It's all I got."

"Gimme the bills." Jeff shook his head. "You'll owe me."

Todd handed them over, reached for the Polaroid—and Jeff grabbed it and grinned.

"Just give it."

"Awful edgy today, Toddie. What, not enough pie from the waitress?"

Todd snatched the Polaroid, walked out, got in the Dart. Held the door shut by hand while driving to a space a block from The Chili Cafe. Hid behind the dash as Fitzie's Dodge passed, got out, ran to the Dumpster behind the cafe. The window was open but too high. Unless he stood on the Dumpster, which was too far. He pushed: nothing. Maybe someone could help. Maybe a kid, but these days kids talked. He shouldered the Dumpster and shoved. Shoved harder, farted, and it rolled. He climbed and peered in: Ned sitting beside a stainless steel table removing a cig from a hardpack—of Marlboros.

Ned smoked, finished smoking and chopped an onion. Then he smoked, scratched his head, smoked, opened a can of beans the size of a live-bucket, smoked, cleared his throat and smoked while sitting on a stool reading the newspaper. He gets paid for this, Todd thought.

Ned's hand began rubbing his thigh. He was reading the comics. Blondie. Then his finger began tapping his crotch. Touching him*self* in new ways, Todd thought. An Arvy suggestion in volume two?

Ned squeezed his crotch and unzipped. Where's Gwen? Todd thought, and Ned removed his penis. It wasn't that big. Then it was. Twice as long as

Todd's but thin, almost eel-like. Ned pinched it, massaged it and, stroking it, walked to the stove. Steam rose; chili bubbled; Ned stroked away. Todd raised the camera. Come on, Gwen, he thought. Ned stroked fast as hummingbird wings, aimed the head up—and squirts lurched and arched into the chili.

Like a fountain, Todd thought. The shutter, he realized, had snapped. Out hissed the photo. Had the noise been too loud? Ned wasn't looking. He was putting himself away. His image was developing, blurry hand first. Todd tossed the photo and re-aimed the camera: Ned zipping, stirring chili, the door to the front opening, Gwen walking in.

"Ready?" she asked.

As ever, Todd thought.

"I suppose," Ned said. He grabbed a red rag, wiped the side of the pot.

"Then bring it out for Christ sake. Those kids are set to act up again."

"Alright already," Ned said.

"And watch the front for once. I'm going to call Sally and tell her to come in."

"We're that busy?"

"No. I want to go home."

"To see Little Toddie?"

"Just bring out the damned extra-hot. I'm sick of your shit." Gwen shoved open the door and was gone.

They're not fucking, Todd thought.

Ned lit up, pulled on silver oven mitts, lifted the pot, backed out through the doorway. Rich kids, Todd thought, are going to eat sperm.

And when Gwen brings it home, so will I.

No problem, he thought. Get Chinese to-go and beat her home. He hopped off the Dumpster, ran to the Dart, got in, tossed the camera and cranked the screwdriver: nothing. And I'm down to twelve cents, he thought. You can't get a potsticker for twelve cents.

The liver.

He got out, kicked the steering wheel, slid in and cranked. That sonofabitch *squirts,* he thought, and the Dart started. He held onto the wheel to stay in during the U-turn, accelerated down Main. No cops. At least some-one trusted. What if someone had seen him taking the picture? Or found it and dusted for prints? He pulled into Gwen's space, threw it in park, ran up and in and opened the freezer. The liver, in plastic, sat as alone as he felt. He grabbed it and tossed it into the sink. The hot water felt cold and grew warm far too slowly. Like Gwen, he thought, and he opened the faucet all the way—and spray soaked his face, neck and shirt. Water dripped from his nose; one eye couldn't see; he blinked and groped and shut off the faucet. Massaged the liver without progress. Jammed it under an armpit, then inside his pants, and rubbed it faster than he would if insane. Heard her Gremlin barrelling home—with that jism-laced chili. The liver was warmer, but he was already fucked: She was coming. She was coming. She was coming.

Birdie

irst day of practice my senior year, I walk out of the locker room and see what looks like a sixth grade white dude whooshing in a jumper from way past the free throw line.

"Who's the punk with the freshies?" I yell across the gym to Shannette.

Shannette and I are buds 'cause we the only two seniors on varsity who don't play—and the only two who'll admit we like to fool around with dudes.

"Transfer," she say. She hit the bottom of the rim with a lay-up. "From California."

"What he doing shooting with the freshies?" I ask. "Managing?"

Shannette put a ball on her hip, squeak her Air Jordans my way and stick her mouth so close to my ear it almost tickle. "SHE," she whisper. "She on the freshy team. Name's Birdie."

A shot HOOSH in on the freshies' side of the gym, and there's this little Birdie, standing thirty feet out, waving a perfect follow-through at the glass blackboard.

"She won't do that again," I say, and someone pass Birdie one of them cheap, worn-down rubber balls, and she hits. I pretend I'm not watching and she hits again, this time from a foot past the three point line. I look at Shannette and she don't say anything. She don't have to. Because lots of girls can shoot, but they mostly have SETTERS, not jumpers, and this Birdie's jumper be like an NBA ESPN highlight, with the elbow under the ball, and the release at the top of the jump, and that perfect backspin you wish you could watch in slow motion.

Two weeks into our regular season, Boys' Varsity starts coming to practice early to watch us scrimmage the freshies. Birdie be rainbowing home twenty-foot jumpers and Boys' Varsity be jumping and hollering like German shepherds under a ham bone hanging from monkey bars. All of us on Girls' Varsity be busting butt on defense and making three-quarter-court bounce passes connect clean on full-speed fast breaks, but Boys' Varsity never cheer for any of that—they just sit there eyeing Birdie, waiting for her to sting in another jay. I gotta admit I was jealous—because I knew Boys' Varsity liked Birdie because she played hoop and looked most like they did. She walked pigeon-toed like them, and had her brown hair cut short like Danny Ainge. The hair on her legs needed shaving more than she bothered with it, you could see the muscles in her little forearms move when she dribbled, and her chest was flat as a back alley.

Which most of Girls' Varsity wasn't. Most of Girls' Varsity had big breasts bouncing everywhere, slowing us down, getting in the way of our shots—at least that be my excuse.

Birdie never made excuses herself. In fact, she hardly even TALKED. When she did it surprised you, sounding low and hoarse and soft. I never heard her say anything until after the practice Shannette's ankle busted and Coach moved Birdie up to Varsity. We played Yates the next day and Coach put in Birdie and HOOSH-HOOSH-HOOSH-HOOSH—she drain four nothing-but-net jumpers in a row. We win by thirty, and after the buzzer to end the game, when we in line doing soft high-fives with the Yates players, their little Mexican point-guard tell Birdie she look like Michael J. Fox.

"Fuck you," Birdie say.

Coach, who the only dude coach in the conference, hear Birdie say this but just laugh. Then he stay up in the Yates Athletic Director's office talking to the Yates coach: the prettiest lady coach in our conference. We go down to the visitors' locker-room and Yolanda, our back-up center, tell us Coach be trying to talk his way into a date up there. She tell us she's sure he'll be in that AD office for at least a half hour, and that she herself's gonna show us how to have fun. She grab some towels and cover the drains on the shower room floor, then turn on all the showers full blast. She yell, "ANYONE COME IN HERE I'LL SPANK THEIR ASS," and stand by the shower room entrance till the steam get thick. When all we can see of her is two bug-bitten feet swooshing water three inches deep over the tile, she step out of the steam and lather up her walking-stick-skinny bones with this itty bitty piece of Dial soap, and say, "Watch this." She disappear between two rows of lockers for a few seconds, then ZOOM out from between them and dive onto the water, sliding arms-first across the shower room floor, laughing her ass off like she had ass to spare.

We all whoop it up and give high and low fives, and then we all sprinting and sliding—and screaming and laughing so hard we can't breathe. Rita, who start at center, be sliding ass-first cause she worried her big old pancake nipples might burn against the tile; she leave a big WAKE behind her, like she a BOAT or something. Watching her slide cracks me up so much I don't care that she makes out with girls and I'm sitting there spread-eagle naked, and all of a sudden this locker slams real hard, which usually means COACH.

Everyone stop where they are, as if we all frozen in that steam, then start cranking the water cooler and acting like we just in there showering, trying to laugh without making any noise, trying to just breathe, hoping Coach won't know we were horseplaying and make us run windsprints next practice.

We don't hear Coach's voice, or ANYTHING from the locker-room doorway, and then the steam get thin, and there, standing near the shower room doorway, is BIRDIE, the big white towel she always brought from home wrapped tight around her little white body.

"Good game, Bird," Rita say from the steam. Rita be showering across from me, water running off her lips, chest heaving, eyes staring at Birdie. I look back at Birdie, but Birdie be gone—and then Yolanda start an ass-stinging towel fight.

Two games later, Birdie start at off-guard, and she nail in ten jumpers easy as blinking. We played Willowridge that game and there wasn't one white face in the crowd except Birdie's squeeze, who was one of them ratty-looking computer nerds; I first thought he was Birdie's twin brother. Birdie DID have a twin but he live in California with Birdie's divorced mom—at least that's what Shanette heard from Yolanda.

Birdie's man DID kind of look like Birdie, though, and WAS a nerd. He never even held her hand at school, just watched her play hoop and gave her rides home in his daddy's new Chevy 4 x 4. Anyway Birdie rained in 28 against Willowridge, and after that game our whole team be standing around the Coke machine waiting for Coach to come out of the Willow-ridge AD office, hoping he would tell us practice would be late the next morning, and Karita—who didn't start because Birdie did, and who, accord-ing to Shannette, DEFINITELY like to make out with girls—say to Birdie, "Your nerd boyfriend any good at the dirty deed?"

Everyone there get quiet. Birdie cross her arms, then open her little mouth and say, "Is there any reason you can't find out for yourself?"

Karita just STAND there, like she just heard her grandaddy got hit by a truck and died, and the rest of the team laugh this loud, nervous laugh. I slap Birdie's back like me and her are old buds, 'cause I'm glad she ain't stupid about how Karita like girls, and 'cause she, little Birdie, just helped us win Conference.

We won District two weeks later, easy—and then Regionals a week after that. Birdie averaged twenty-eight in those games, but then of course, like every year, came State.

In Texas, girls play State in Austin, in the Auditorium where the UT Men play the Southwest Conference and Clarissa Davis and some other Women Olympics players used to hoop. My freshy, sophomore and junior years, we got to go there the night before and stay in the Austin Holiday Inn, but this time the district had run out of money, so we had to climb into this nasty old yellow school bus at SIX IN THE MORNING GAME DAY, and ride all the way there without stopping. Two hours after all that sitting, we be out there, under the too-bright TV lights, feeling raggedy as the wet chickens Mr. Sherman hatched in Biology, all of us quiet except for the squeak of our Nikes on that sweet, refinished floor. I missed my first four layups, nervous as shit 'cause even though it's still the semi-finals, we about to play #1 Duncanville. We, according to what Shannette's mom saw in the paper the night before, are ranked #3. Earlier that day #2 Odessa lost the other semi-final game to some Pee Wee San Antonio team 'cause Odessa's 38-point-a-game forward had mono, so our game coming up pretty much WAS the championship; whoever won would just show up the next day and walk out holding those big gold trophies over they heads.

After I miss my four layups, I can't hardly breathe; I had to pee real bad and was sweating like a horse for no reason. Birdie, though, look cool. She wasn't even warming up; she just stand at half court like she on some empty playground, looking at Duncanville like they weren't called DUNKville, which everyone called them because their center could actually do it. She be Black but must be from some other country 'cause she at least six-seven and have a BIG OLD BUTT—she probably never saw a theatre movie without having to sit in the aisle.

The horn to start the game sounded like a siren only it stayed on forever—when the state tournament dude flipped it off I felt deaf. Except I could hear the crowd talking. I couldn't see any faces but could feel them all around me; I almost fainted as I sat on the bench. And I wasn't even supposed to PLAY. Fact was, as much as I like to play hoop, I was glad I was sitting. Just win one more, I kept thinking; I wanted to say that to the starters but I knew it would make them nervous. I almost said it to Shannette but didn't because she was in her own other world: on the bench next to me with her ankle just out of its cast—her mom called Coach two nights earlier and threatened to call the principal if Shannette couldn't sit on the bench after being on the team three years and breaking her ankle.

Of COURSE the game was tight. Straight through—you hoped for that ten point lead but it just wouldn't happen. If we scored, Dunkville scored. If they missed, so did we. No more than a three point lead for anyone all the way to the fourth quarter, when everybody be so tired from playing defense it come down to Miss BIG BUTT against Birdie. BIG BUTT step in the lane, they lob the ball to her, she turn around and lay it in. Birdie use a double screen, we bounce it to her, she stroke up a jumper that rain home. Lob to BIG BUTT: two. Screen for Birdie: TWO. Back and forth like that—they up one, we up one. The crowd be capacity but the seats all be empty 'cause everyone standing and twirling letter jackets and screaming like they lungs coming out of they nostrils. When there's fifty-seven seconds left I'm watching the clock through my fingers, thinking PLEASE God let us have the ball last, hoping we can set one more double screen for Birdie before she foul out with her fifth. Then it's down to eighteen seconds and we up 42-41 and Dunkville's point guard is dribbling. She lob it in to Big Butt. TWO. The Dunkville crowd scream so loud I dig my nails into my face. Birdie dribble up court and run into this Dunkville forward, who fall down and bounce up and run past our bench yelling "I FELT IT! I FELT IT!" at this skinny little homeboy-looking ref.

Homeboy ref lower his ear toward this Dunkville forward's yapping-away mouth, then blow his whistle and walk his tiny ass to the scorer's table.

"FELT *WHAT?*" Shannette yell, right in my ear.

"SHUT UP!" I yell back—I'm trying to hear Homeboy, who's yelling something to someone behind the scorer at the table.

"THAT WASN'T NO FOUL!" Shannette say. She got her hands on her head and I realize mine are set to choke my own throat. Coach get up and walk to the table; the Dunkville coach run out there and stand behind Coach. Homeboy blow his whistle and call an official time-out, Birdie standing out on that sweet floor, sweating from her upper lip, all of us subs keeping our butts on the bench to avoid a technical foul, stretching our necks to hear what Homeboy is saying to Coach—which we can't. Then Dunkville's coach, this white dude with a head shaped like a peanut, start talking to the old bald ref in the jump circle, and all these tournament dudes wearing three-piece-suits walk onto the court ruining it with their blacksoled street shoes. The horn go on; the horn go off; the old bald ref wave at Coach and move his head just a little, like he's telling Coach, "Come over here."

And Coach go. He give the Dunkville coach a dirty look and the crowd boo and the old bald ref grab Coach's elbow and start shouting in Coach's ear, pointing at Birdie.

Coach shout back so hard his neck veins get fat, and I say "THEY FOULING HER OUT" without looking at anyone.

"FOR WHAT?" Shannette say.

Coach stomp back to our bench and the old bald ref follow yelling, "DID SHE HAVE IT IN CALIFORNIA OR IN TEXAS?"

"HAVE WHAT?" Shanette yell—and I cover her mouth with my hand to prevent a tech.

"SHE HAD IT IN CALIFORNIA," coach yell at the ref.

"THE RULES SAY SHE HAS TO HAVE IT IN TEXAS," the ref tell him. "IF SHE HASN'T HAS IT IN TEXAS, SHE CAN'T PLAY." He walk toward the scorer's table, and Coach follow, arguing and yanking his own hair. SPIT be spraying out of his mouth and the crowd on both sides boo louder. Pepsi cups start flying, and some hit the court, and after the court's glistening from ice the announcer come on and say, "ANYONE WHO GET CAUGHT THROW-ING ANYTHING WILL GET ARRESTED." Then MORE cups fly down, and then pennies, and then dimes and quarters, too. Both refs' mouths be flapping in Coach's ear, and then Coach throw up his hands and walk toward me and Shannette shaking his head. Shannette start standing and I yank her ass down; the lights feel hotter and a cup of something orange just misses Yolanda. Then a big old APPLE core hit the old bald ref on the shoe, which he pretend he don't see—but the crowd laugh anyway. Coach is standing ten feet from our bench, staring at Shannette. He use his finger to call Birdie over to the top of the three point circle, and Birdie walk over, pigeon-toed, sweating but cool. Coach put his arm around her and start talking in her ear, both he and her serious and blinking, the crowd chanting BYE-BYE BIRDIE, BYE-BYE BIRDIE, Birdie listening to Coach with her eyes on our hoop and her hands on her hips, the little muscles in her wrists squeezing tight-loose-tight-loose, her mouth getting smaller and smaller like it might shrink right off her face.

Then Coach stop talking, and just look at her. She stand there shifting her weight from one foot to the other, staring at the hoop, eyes glistening like the ice melting on the floor around her, little mouth not going anywhere but not saying anything either, 5,000 people screaming like she's some kind of little white Michael Jackson.

Then she nod. She keep looking at the hoop but she nod, just once. Coach lift his head and eyeball the whole bench. His eyes run back and forth until they stop on mine; he lift his finger and move it to call me out there. I point at the out-of-bounds line we can't cross unless we report in to a ref. Coach look at the bald ref and the bald ref give me the nod. I walk out there thinking GIRL, this is your CHANCE. Coach watch me walk as if he suddenly my daddy; Birdie be staring at our rim, only kind of mean now, eyes not sparkling, just watching that orange hoop like it's the only thing there.

Then the old bald ref grab Birdie's elbow, and Coach grab mine, and the old bald ref lead us all past the scorer's table with that peanut-head Dunkville coach following. We all pass the Dunkville bench and the extra folding chairs; I think WHERE ARE WE GOING? and then we're out from under the lights. I glance up once and see all those faces clearly, multiplied by two makes 10,000 eyes watching us walk toward one of them little lit red signs that says EXIT. We go under the sign and down this ramp, and then we in this hallway that's quiet and empty except for popcorn spilling out of a popcorn maker like it's sitting on a pack of lit firecrackers.

The old bald ref open a door and we all follow him in; it's a locker-room with ref shirts and clothes hanging in three lockers.

Coach close the door behind me and say, "This is absolutely ridiculous."

The old bald ref say, "It's our only recourse if she wants to finish the game. This is the fourth report we've had of suspicion." He lead Birdie to this all-dressed-up white lady by the sinks, and Birdie stop there, and we all stop and stand behind her.

The white lady put her hand on Birdie's shoulder and say, "I'm Dr. Connelly. I think it's important that we all relax."

Birdie look over her shoulder at Coach. "Here?" she say.

"Only if you want to," Coach say.

"I don't want to," Birdie say.

"Then the game's under protest," the old bald ref say.

"What's going on?" I say.

"We need you here to watch this," the old bald ref say.

"Watch what?" I say.

Then Birdie yank down her shorts. She stand there looking in the mirror, wearing nothing but her jersey and white panties. Coach and the Dunkville coach and the old bald ref take a few steps away, and pace back and forth facing the far wall. Birdie's eyes look bored and pissed at the same time, but then her chin crinkle like she might cry, and she all at once yank down her panties.

"Birdie?" I say, and the lady doctor crouch down beside her. "I'm sorry, Birdie," the lady doctor say, with her voice a lot higher than before. "But I can't quite see because of the shadow." She clear her throat. "Can you open," she say, "your legs?"

Birdie cross her arms loosely and half-open her legs. There's hardly any hair between them, and there's not any female love lips, but there's not any guy stuff either. There's just this THING, this pink thing shaped like a clit but almost as long as my finger—I once saw something a little like it in the freak chapter of Shannette's mom's medical book. This thing scare me at first but then it make me feel sorry, because I can't imagine it ever doing anything wrong, can't imagine it ever even touching anyone anywhere, because it just sort of hang there, making me wonder, kind of shy-looking—like Birdie.

The Work I've Invested

*I*n the better days, Larry, the neutered gray poodle Ron received from his third divorce settlement, led Ron on rhythmic, zigzagging journeys from tree to tree in Central Park. Now Ron stood on last summer's leaves, observing their decay, holding Larry's leash—without Larry. Therapy is sado-masochism, he thought. Holding a dogless leash is belittling.

Three Minute Mike approached from Columbus Circle. Three Minute Mike always talked for three minutes. He never asked about Ron. Sometimes Mike was funny, but today he wouldn't be. Today Ron's memories—of his ex-wives and Larry—meant no one would be.

"Ron," Three Minute Mike yelled.

Ron gazed at the end of the leash.

"Ron!"

Ron looked up. Three Minute Mike was wearing his magenta jogging outfit, Buddy Rich grin and extra-thick stolen gold jewelry. He glanced at the leash and got in his stance, hands set to gesture. "You wouldn't believe what happened to me yesterday, Ron. I go jogging around the Reservoir, and after six miles I'm sweating, so I take off my shirt, and all these women start staring at me."

"No need to yell, Mike."

"And one of them stops walking to stare, so I stop jogging, and we get to talking, and—right off—she asks, 'What do you do?'"

"Uh-huh."

"I hate how women ask that right off. It's like they judge men by nothing but earning potential. So I tell this woman, 'You women all judge men by nothing but earning potential. And you're so obvious about it. You have no social skills whatsoever.' And—check this out—she calls me a jerk and walks off."

Ron cleared his throat. "A woman with nerve."

"So I go home, shower, call my buddy Toby, and we go out drinking. And there's these two women at O'Donohue's, and Toby starts talking with the better-looking one, so I'm standing next to the other one, and—*right* off—she asks what I do."

One minute, Ron thought.

"So *I* ask, 'What does it matter?' And she says, 'I was just trying to make conversation.' And I say, 'You're making me feel like you wouldn't date me unless I had money.' And she says, 'I wouldn't date you if you won the Publisher's Clearinghouse—because you're obviously an obnoxious jerk.' So I say, 'You obviously have no social skills.' And *she* walks away."

In the better days, Ron realized, Larry would pull. Poor Larry, Ron thought. The poor leaves, the poor grass, the poor monarchs that had to fly south.

"Then Toby comes up and says, 'Way to go.' And I say, 'What do you mean?' And he says, 'I was doing great with that looker and the woman you were with came up and said she wanted to go to the China Club.'"

Ron stared at the chewed part of the leash. I do have those teeth marks, he thought. Which lead to the memories, which might be the cause of my problem. But happiness—by the time you feel it—is based on memories as well.

"Are you listening to me, Ron?"

"Yes. The China Club."

"Do you care what happens next?"

"I know what happens next. The women go to the China Club."

"And you know that because you've been in my shoes. But check this out. As soon as they leave, *Toby* tells me I'm obnoxious—and *he* leaves."

Memories aren't my problem, Ron thought. My problem is not wanting to share them.

"So I order a bourbon and start telling the barkeep how the average woman these days has no social skills. And he says, 'The average woman these days is about as self-absorbed as you.' And he walks to the other end of the bar and watches TV by himself. Can you believe that?"

"I guess I have to, Mike."

"You and me both. So then I'm nursing this bourbon, and I start telling the women who ask me for matches to call me The Prophet. And they say, 'What do you mean?' And I say, 'I'm like a saint or something.' And they say, 'Really?' And I say, 'I'm like one of those martyrs. I'm fated never to marry. I've been put on earth to tell women to improve their social skills before the species goes extinct.'"

"Did they go for that?"

"Who."

"The women who asked you for matches."

"One did. But she had a glass eye. I tell you, Ron, it was a helluva night."

"Sounds like it kept coming at you."

"It did. When I got home I called one of those phone sex girls, and when I finally got her clothes off, she said she had to hang up to call her Aunt Gertrude in Arkansas."

"Horrible," Ron said.

"Horrible *social* skills, Ron." Three Minute Mike squinted at the sky. "I think I'll go jogging with my shirt off again." He walked off, glanced over his shoulder and yelled, "If you see me, call me The Prophet."

Like an eggtimer, Ron thought.

A woman approached from Columbus Circle. Her hair was bleached white and she wore a purple sequined belly dancing outfit, and the sun seemed to shine on her only. Breast implants, Ron guessed as she drew closer, were one-upping the lift of her Wonderbra. "Spring's around the corner, huh?" she said.

"I imagine," Ron said.

"Where's your pooch?"

"My therapist told me to do this." Ron raised the leash. "To help me cope with losing him."

"He ran off?"

"We were waiting for a WALK sign on 72nd and Broadway. He took one step down—and it was over."

Ron pictured Larry lying beside the sewer on 72nd.

"You're not much of a talker, are you?" the woman asked.

"Not recently."

"You seem like a loner."

"I feel just the opposite."

"Yet you use very few words. I had a boyfriend like that. He was an Arab—I met him at a gig I was doing at this after-hours Arabian men's club—and he hardly ever said more than three words at a time. He had these imported CD's of this wonderful Arabian music, though, and he'd ask me to bellydance to them, and after I would—to a whole CD—he'd put on another CD and ask me to *keep* dancing. Which I'd usually do because I love my dancing. But when I'd dance for this guy, he'd stare at me. Continuously. As if I were at his …"

"Disposal?"

"That was my word! Anyway, I got tired of his staring. See, I'm a feminist—during the day I work for this wonderful new lesbian magazine. And he *knew* that. Yet he'd continue to stare at me, as if bellydancing were some sort of … striptease. Men can be unbearably selfish, you know what I mean?"

"Yes."

"This other one I went out with was a freelance photographer for this magazine. I met him at this bellydancing contest I won, and we went out a few times, and he seemed nice enough, so I decided to do this shoot he and this magazine set up for me. So he takes these beautiful pictures of me in various stages of undress—actually it was the totally nude ones that were gorgeous."

Larry's leash touched trampled sod.

"I mean those pictures were *art*. And the magazine wanted to run them, only they airbrushed them to make me look like an object—which, of course, I hated. They offered me $50,000, though. All I had to do was sign a release and a contract. Just write my name twice."

"Did you?"

"Are you *kidding?* I'm a feminist for God's sake! Plus I know these bellydancers who've been in X-rated films, and they can't get bellydancing parts in full-length feature films because they've got reputations as porno princesses. My point is, is it worth it? Do I want to obliterate my career? Especially after all the work I've invested in myself? I mean, I won an absolutely wonderful $3,000 silk bellydancing costume in this competition in Morocco—this costume is *gorgeous*—and I've danced professionally in Las Vegas three times, and the hotel manager I dated there says he'll hire me back whenever I want. I mean, who wants to mess with a known quantity?"

"I see."

"Do you really?"

Ron pictured Larry yanking the leash toward a trail no one but Ron cared to follow. "I do," he said, admitting his skill at divorce. "I definitely see what you're saying."

Double Bad

W e made love like the student-athletes we were, with quick moves, good hands and the ability to change pace. Gwen, I'll admit, had better wind. She knew when to take her time-outs. We finished, as they say, simultaneously.

"Don't say I was good," she said. "Everyone says that."

I yawned. "You were horrible." I wanted to distinguish myself because, at a party hours earlier, she'd been arm-in-arm with the baseball team's third baseman—Ron—when she'd suggested I'd visit her dorm. I didn't like Ron but acted as if I did: that's how I was around jocks. In her room, she'd kissed first. Now she was kissing my navel. Our smells, on me, seemed to fuel her.

"I can't," I said.

"Push yourself."

I tried, which felt like overtime. Then, as in overtime, I managed, operating on pride, obstinacy and adrenaline. She stopped and started until I passed out. It was one of those marathon sleeps that takes you to the last slice of the next day. I lay awake for minutes before I remembered the party. She, near the edge of the bed, was still out. I wanted to get sun—or what was left of it—but didn't want to ghost her. I had morals of sorts. This was a Catholic college in Texas. Finally, she stirred. Her eyes shot toward the clock. "We missed a day," I said.

Her silence relaxed me. Then she asked, "What do you do to cure hangovers?"

"Sweat."

"I can't fuck more. I'm sore."

"I didn't say fuck. I meant run."

"I can't move."

"Then sleep." I found my jockeys and cut-off shorts, slid them on, found my T-shirt, pulled it over me inside out.

"You're leaving?"

"I gotta sweat this out of me." I stepped into my shoes and she got out of bed and walked toward her closet. Her legs appeared longer than they had the night before, her breasts softer. She was nearly six feet with the musculature of a man, the bone structure of a pre-pubescent girl. She slid on baggy yellow gym shorts, pulled on a navy blue sweatshirt that, in red letters inside a green circle, read MANHATTAN BEACH CLUB. "I thought you couldn't move," I said.

"I'm going with."

"Don't do me any favors."

She slipped on her shoes, found her keys and, shoes unlaced, led me out of the room, down the hall and to the elevator, then through the lobby and into a peculiar evening. Eighty degrees only two days into March, a lip of black clouds stuck on the eastern horizon. She walked ahead of me, toward the gym, where probably, in the basement, the baseball team was pumping iron.

"I do it outside," I called. "At this junior high playground."

"We need a ball." She held up a key, apparently to the equipment room. How had she gotten it—screwed the equipment manager? "I wanna shoot. There's a hoop there, right?"

I nodded and caught up, then figured the baseball team would give us crap, and I didn't want to deal with that. I stopped on the stairs to the gym.

"What's wrong?"

"I thought you were getting a ball."

She shrugged and went in. It was as if, between her bed and the gym, we'd gotten engaged and grown bored. I faced the sun and let it burn. She was on my nostrils, which I liked, but mostly I wanted to sweat. I had this theory about cleanliness: sun-induced sweat worked better than showering. When you showered, oil repelled water, thus requiring soap, which, as those television ads taught, left a film. On the other hand, sweat flushed out pores—and sunshine burned and tightened them closed. Other than this theory, I wasn't a nature freak. Leather sneakers, hamburgers, the use of mice to cure AIDS—none of that bothered me.

I sat on a stair and lay back. The campus was empty: dinnertime. I thought about how easy everything was: shooting, passing, defense, home-work, midterms, getting laid. People off campus were getting divorced, audited and car-jacked, but not me. In two months I'd graduate, which would also be easy. The Deans wanted me to stay *cum laude;* they kept my GPA high. And I'd get a cake job because alumni loved jocks. Would it remain easy? I shut my eyes and aimed my shins at the sun.

Where was Gwen? Probably, I imagined, flirting with Ron. I didn't get flirtation. If you want sex, I believed then, have it. Otherwise why pretend? Still, people teased. They needed the show. I opened my eyes, ignored a cheerleader's hello, closed them. Cheerleaders irked me. Where was Gwen? My left calf twitched, in need of exercise. Had Gwen joined me so she could flirt? If so, I faced rudeness. And the rude never respected the tolerant; elbows under the basket stopped only when *you* elbowed. To hit the junior high myself, I decided, would be wise.

I stood. Though shooting with her, I thought, might be fun. I faced the gym and folded my arms. Waiting, I knew from childhood, was what spouses did; a significant portion of marriage involved patience and atrophy. Then it hit me that maybe she'd wanted me with her. She'd wanted to show me off to Ron?

I pictured the supply closet down the hall from the weight room. The light in there didn't work, and I pictured Ron and her alone in that darkness. Double-entendres, laughter, mutual admiration of the whiteness of their teeth. Shorts slid down faster than blue jeans; quickies, quite often, were best.

"Hey," she said behind me, in the doorway. Ron, beside her, flashed me the grin he gave pitchers after hitting their best stuff for home runs. He's got it for her, I thought. Bad. I stood, stretched, and walked off. Gwen gained to stay within a step of me. I faced The Choice: ask her why she'd taken so long or play like I didn't care. I'd never been the type to ask. If they fuck behind your back, I'd always believed, they'll never be the type to admit it.

Then our silence was only making me older. "Took awhile," I said.

"I was just shooting the shit."

I knew The Rule: Ask whom with, but no more. Instead I jogged off. If she followed me, fine. Either way, I'd sweat and feel sunshine. She accelerated to grow even, her stride coordinated but gangly: forced athleticism to show me, I imagined, that she, too, would play hoop until she graduated. She had three years left, though. She couldn't see the end. When you see the end, you admit how spoiled jocks are.

We reached the junior high and she angled off to shoot. I lapped the track twice, stopped for sun, sprinted around twice and joined her. We played horse without laughing. The ball was flat too. Then we jogged back to campus, wordless, and the sun was behind the cedar trees, and I didn't know where to go.

"Shower?" she said as she began for her dorm.

"You mean together?"

"You want to?"

"I don't know," I said. "Up to you."

She opened the lobby door and walked in. I didn't want to follow but did. I didn't like her, which might have meant I loved her.

"What you thinking?" she asked.

"Nothing." We were riding the elevator, the ball on her hip. We got off on 2, passed an open doorway: 3 sophomores feigning nonchalance in nothing but bras and panties. Gwen, ahead, opened her door and, frowning, nodded for me to close it.

"Why you so quiet?" she asked inside.

"You're the quiet one."

"You haven't said jack since I left the gym."

She wants jealousy, I thought. She needs it?

"It's like while I was in there, you changed," she said.

"Maybe *you* changed."

"What's that supposed to mean?"

"It means. Maybe. You. Changed."

"How would getting a basketball make me change?"

"Maybe someone with you changed you."

"What in hell are you talking about?"

"Someone in the equipment room." Dumbshit, I thought. Shouldn't have said that.

"Listen, Mr. Macho. I don't owe you a thing. But I like you, so to humor you, I'll tell you he didn't touch me down there."

"Don't humor me."

"Fine." She glared, sour-faced.

"You were down there forever."

"I was getting. A basketball."

"For half an hour?"

"I had to inflate it. He showed me how, okay?"

"You didn't know *how?* Anyway, that ball's flat."

"No it's not."

"Yes it is. We just shot with it, for Christ's sake." I reached for the ball and she hid it behind her.

"It's not flat, okay?"

"Then give it to me."

"No."

"Then dribble it."

"Why don't you get the hell out of here?"

I sat on her bed. I stood and walked out. To prevent rape in that dorm, men were supposed to be escorted by women, so a redhead in a lime green nightgown offered to ride the elevator with me. "Thanks, no," I said, and she came anyway. Her nipples were obvious through lime green lace, and she gazed at the numbers to let me glance—probably only because I played ball. As we rode, I neither glanced nor spoke. I was tired of the hero-worship, the gossip, the ante-up of egos. The ways of the elite disgusted and bored me. I preferred my lot during my last two summers in high school, when I'd done maintenance in a factory. I'd had to wheel a grimy cart to 29 work stations and empty forty gallon drums of steel filings into it, and the old-timers, who didn't know I played ball, ridiculed me.

In the lobby, security nodded as I left. The old-timers, I realized, had made me feel real. The sky was dark, maybe 6:45. My dorm was across the baseball field on which Ron practiced, so I didn't want to step on it. Still, I began across it. Nor did I want to return to my room: my teammates would force me to drink. I was tired of drinking. We were apprentice alcoholics and no one cared. A step from third base, I pictured Ron's hand in those baggy yellow shorts, and I veered. Then my dorm loomed. I stopped and turned. Gwen's window, the last on the right on the second floor of her dorm, was lit. I told myself not to return, then felt trapped despite being outdoors. Details became clear: textbooks on shelves, a potted cactus, her life-sized poster of Andre Agassi. But no Gwen. Was she lying on her bed? By herself or with Ron? I shuffled toward her dorm and stopped in shallow right-center; if she appeared at the window, I didn't want her to see me. Yet I had to see her. I was jealous, no better than the pettiest cheerleader. I stood watching the window, feeling a sociopath's shame but no thrill. I sat down. For a moment, my stillness felt right. Then headlights appeared on the driveway through campus; I lay on my back, heard the car pass, sat up and continued to spy. What if a prof saw and asked what I was doing? If my English prof knew, he'd call me sexist.

Then someone blipped past the window. Ron, I thought. If so, matters would have been easier. The figure reappeared, Gwen smoking a cigarette. I hadn't known her to smoke, but the sight didn't surprise me. Forget her, I thought. She'll get cancer anyway. Then I considered marriage to the very best woman in the world. If she'd die first, grief would hollow me; if I would, she'd replace me easily. I stood, sighed, began toward Gwen. She disappeared and my momentum confused me. Then I had it figured. I needed to win or lose. Standing out there had been half-time.

"You'll need an escort," the guard in the lobby said.

"But you know me."

"Don't matter."

In three years, I'd never needed an escort. Had Gwen phoned the desk? "I'll take him," a voice said: the redhead in the green nightgown, beside the elevator, forearms over her chest. Where had she been? In the TV room. Watching me watch Gwen through its window?

"Thanks," I said. In the elevator, as we ascended, I noticed she'd bleached hairs on the side of her face. I began to like her. She was never at parties—probably didn't even sip beer.

"Here we are," she said as the doors opened. "Two, right?"

"Yeah." I gestured for her to lead.

"I'm not getting off."

"Oh."

I blushed, strode out, and stood at Gwen's door. I checked both ways, then tried to eavesdrop. Nothing. Those headlights were Ron's? I wondered. Catch them, I thought, and I opened the door. She was facing the window, guzzling Milk Duds from a large box. I passed Andre Agassi, knelt at her bed, looked beneath it.

"What're you doing?"

I parted blouses in her closet. "Nothing."

"I fucked him," she said.

"Who."

"Ron."

I stepped into her bathroom, pulled back the shower curtain.

"I said I fucked him."

"I heard you."

"Then what are you doing?"

"I don't know." I was searching only because I'd *been* searching. "You tell me." I sat on the edge of the toilet.

"I fuck guys," she called. "Because I want to fuck well. If the fact that I fuck bugs someone I've fucked, I fuck someone else. I've done 36 guys on this campus not including t.a.'s. I did my cousin in his truck bed in my parents' garage. I'm up to 72 total, 64 if you don't count oral."

Truth, I thought. After sex.

"Anything you don't do?" I called.

"Women."

"Why not?"

"I hate how they smell. Which, yeah, probably means I hate myself, but, you know, if you want to save a slut, find yourself one with a heart."

I poked my head out the bathroom doorway. She puffed smoke, pressed her cigarette into sand beside the cactus and covered her face with her hands. Then I went out there. I kissed the backs of her fingers. You don't want to do this, I told myself. You have to. I kissed her hairline, her neck, her T-shirt; I touched the tight skin between her breasts. Foreplay with her, I realized, was like trying out for a coach: you had to prove skills before she allowed you to perform under her control.

Her eyes, open, followed my hands. "Can you do something for me?" she asked.

"What."

"See someone with me."

"Who."

"I don't know. Someone, you know, like a counselor?"

Absolutely not, I thought as my voice quavered to say, "If you want."

■ ■ ■

Actually there were two counselors, Carlos and Angie, in the closed conference room in the Counseling Center. Carlos was plump but tight, maybe 45; he wore a white guayaberra shirt and rectangular silver glasses over watery eyes that locked onto me while I shook hands with Angie, tiny but solid, maybe 35, with a bad red dye job and a large sebaceous cyst on the left side of a re-done nose.

Angie liked to dress: earrings, necklaces, bangles. "Carlos and I almost divorced," she said as we sat. "After experiencing the dark side. We weren't high on counselling either, so please know we know how you feel."

Carlos' eyes had me pinned. He'd cheated first—I was sure of it. What, I wanted to ask him, if Angie had?

"We're very much in love now," Angie said.

"Thanks to Jesus Christ Our Personal Savior," Carlos said.

"Let's begin by joining hands in prayer," Angie said.

Gwen stood—to leave, I was sure—we'd come for counsel, not prayer—but she squeezed Carlos' left hand as he offered me his right.

"Must I?" I asked.

He froze. His eyes darted between mine and Angie's. She shrugged and took Gwen's free hand, and the three of them lowered their foreheads. Then, as if triple-teaming me, they recited a Hail Mary.

As we sat, he told me, "Don't worry. Being scared is natural."

"I'm not scared," I said. "I'm just not the one with the problem."

"Then why are you here?"

"Because." I leaned back. "She seduced me."

"Is that true?" Angie asked Gwen, who considered the gray carpet, then nodded.

"Okay, Dear," Carlos said. "Why don't you tell us your story?"

Gwen chewed a thumbnail so long I considered a move for the door. Then, from her mouth, flowed a list of sex acts and names. Most of the deeds had been done in cars in an auto supply store parking lot, fewer than half of the men strangers to me. Until Ron, she explained, she'd convinced every partner, as well as her friends, that she'd been a virgin. Her false virginity, in fact, had seduced the ambivalent. It also had kept her partners silent— or so she'd believed. Ron, before he'd raped her in the equipment room while I'd stood outside, was the first to call her bluff, telling her what his friends had said about her experiences with them. While he'd raped her, she'd felt boredom. While she'd shot baskets with me, she'd felt hatred toward me and a fresh crush on Ron. The crush had confused her—how could she like someone who'd raped her? The confusion had forced her to admit to herself that sex with strangers was a sin.

"And holding hands with strangers to say a Hail Mary?" Carlos asked, eyes taking her in.

She breathed out a laugh. "Not a sin."

"How would you characterize it?" Angie asked.

Gwen bit the same thumbnail.

She might hate me, I thought, but she must want us to leave.

"It relaxed me," she said, "more than any kiss, hug, or beer I've ever enjoyed."

Carlos shifted in his chair. "Beautiful," he said.

"Quite," Angie said.

"I'd say … I sense contrition," Carlos said. "You, Dear?"

"I definitely sense contrition," Angie said.

"And you, Dear?" Carlos asked.

Gwen nodded.

"Then our next step," Angie said, "is a blessing for healing." She regarded me as if we were reformed swingers. "Would you agree to a blessing for healing?"

"Sure," I said—to get the hell out of there.

"Then we'll meet tomorrow evening at six. At St. Matthew's."

No way, I thought.

"In the meantime," Carlos told Gwen, "I advise you spend your time away from your friend here."

"Oh?" Angie said.

"For prayer's sake," Carlos said.

■　■　■

An hour before that counselling session I'd convinced myself to quit drinking for good, but after it I figured a beer with the boys wouldn't hurt.

As usual, my suitemates and I began with a case. With four longnecks left, Ron's girlfriend Jane stopped by with tequila. I hate tequila but downed what she offered because, I'll admit, I wanted to get back at Ron. It wasn't like I thought I'd end up with her: Jane simply wasn't like that. It was merely a statement to him—if he walked in and saw us—that I'd always be *there*. That's something about me that still goes today: I don't like to back down.

Anyway I ended up hammered, which was nothing new except, when my suitemates convinced Jane to play Only-Down-to-Undies Strip Poker, I got quiet. Usually, when drunk, I talked more than most, giving shit so bad no one dared give it back, but after they dealt the fourth hand, I lay on my bed and pretended to pass out. I was, I knew, backing down from their game, but I didn't care. I just wanted to call Gwen.

After their voices grew subdued—Jane had removed her blouse—I passed out or fell asleep. I woke to an empty suite and the thought-provoking smell of empty beer cans. I hit the junior high playground myself, did so many laps I lost count, sat in the sun and let the sweat flow. I walked home and showered longer than necessary. I was hungry but didn't want to see Ron or my suitemates in the cafeteria, so I hit a McDonald's. I downed a large Coke and 2 cheeseburgers, my supplementary cure for the hangover, and then it was 5:15.

I would just check the parking lot to see if her dented Volvo was there: that's the thought that sparked my two-mile walk to St. Matthews. The Volvo wasn't there. I turned and began back. Then I told myself I might have been early, and I returned to the lot and stood on its edge like a car thief. The service began—I heard organ chords through St. Matthew's open windows—and I waited for her to arrive late. The sky was cloudless, the sun on my face, so I didn't mind. You were the sucker, I told myself. But at least you didn't back down.

Then I wondered if Carlos and Angie had given her a ride. I jogged to the church door and entered. Toward the front of a line of a dozen people in the center aisle stood Gwen, in a sleeveless white blouse and a knee-length skirt, her hair, more auburn than I'd remembered, piled and bobby-pinned on top of her head. The line, flanked at the very front by Carlos, in a beige guayaberra shirt, and Angie, in a wide plaid dress, consisted largely of octogenarians, one marred by a port wine stain on his chin and neck, several in wheelchairs, a young, pale priest blessing them in turns until each fell backward into Carlos' and Angie's arms.

She's *doing* it? I thought. She can't be. Then the old man in front of her fell, and she stepped forward, and the priest placed his hands on her head. I sat in a pew beside stacked wicker collection baskets and tried to make sense of everything. The priest whispered over her hair, then into her ear. Her folded arms dropped to her sides. She thinks she needs this? I thought, and her knees buckled and she fell backward—Carlos and Angie had her. They prayed over her, laid her beside the altar. They left to attend the next soul in line, and she sat up. Other blessings continued, laced by moans and gasps, but I watched her until she saw me. She smiled and pointed to the end of the line: a fellow jock challenging me to prove bravery?

To humor her, I stood, faked a move toward the altar, and sat down. She smirked, then gazed at the choir loft over my head. Unless I was blessed, I realized, she'd feel conspicuous and ashamed. Do it, I thought. You'll have something in common. At least get in line—you can always turn back.

I stood and walked up there. Grinning, she flashed a thumbs-up. In an hour, I was sure, we would talk, walk and laugh, and whatever we'd say would be true. Two old women, one in a wheelchair, eased into line behind me. In front of me was the bald crown of an old man. Its sheen and pink hue made me want to live forever—and then I was next.

I stepped past Carlos and Angie. Then it was just me and the priest. He assessed me: the youngest man present, unabashed, unafraid to assess him. Because of two stairs that led to the altar, he stood an inch taller than I. He placed his hands on my head. They were soft, the hands of a pianist. He spoke in murmurs about love, evil and forgiveness, about the relationships between life and darkness. His thumbs massaged my forehead, bringing to mind my skin's oiliness. Then I realized he was making tiny signs of the cross. He spoke louder, as if addressing everyone, about fear. His eyes, a glance told me, reflected impatience: I was supposed to relax and go down. But my stance felt strong; squat-thrusts, pick-up games and relative youth had brought me there in the best shape of my life. Don't fight this, I thought. But don't fake a fall. If you do, you'll never believe anything.

Two hands, one smaller than the other, gripped either of my biceps. I looked left: Carlos. "Close your eyes," he said. Into my right ear, Angie was whispering Latin. They pinned my arms against my sides; I realized I was making a scene. Plus the women behind me were more or less on last legs: certainly I was holding up progress. Still, I couldn't fake it. Someone grabbed the back of my head, probably—given the size and boniness of the fingers—one of the old women. Carlos and Angie took hold of my shoulders; the bony fingers pulled back my head until I faced a ceiling mural of St. Jude; the priest's thumb pressed my forehead *firmly,* and then, all at once, it happened. The dynamics of the physics involved in losing leverage and balance, I admitted, feel pretty damned miraculous, and then I was horizontal—and arms panicked to soften my fall.

Interestingly, I felt no shame. My eyes, I realized, were shut. I didn't want to open them, and when I opened them, I didn't want to move. To rise meant dealing with ancient strangers who hovered so close I could smell the musty scents of their homes. They grabbed and lifted my ankles and wrists and placed me beside the priest. I was on unforgiving marble imported from The Vatican or Mexico. Carlos' face appeared, upside-down. He said, "Pray for my forgiveness." What did *that* mean? I nodded to induce him to leave, and his face disappeared. To follow him to the pews meant certain mild embarrassment; to lie there during whatever ceremony followed the blessings would mean the terror of every eye on me.

I sat up. The wheelchair of the last woman in line tilted backward with assistance from Angie. Carlos and the man with the port wine stain were grabbing a wicker basket apiece. In the aisle to the left of the pews, Gwen stood face-to-face with a guy at least two years younger than she, apparently in his counsel. Where, I wondered, had he been earlier? They hugged, chest against breasts. Months later they would marry, but I didn't even suspect that then: my mistrust of her motives, in her mind then, might have required me to endure another blessing. Walk toward them and greet them, I told myself. Forgive her, return to a pew with her, hold her hand while you, she and he renounce evil. Follow the steps that will allow you down the center aisle and out the door as comfortably as possible. Out there, in that white-hot sunshine, let her new sins determine your course.

Confession

I don't want to discuss Joan when she drank. I have to, though,
because what Perney and I did sounds monstrous if you don't know the
whole story.

When Joan drank the hardest—when she met my friend Mayo—she
chugged Johnny Walker in her daddy's Electra while cheating on her high
school boyfriend. Mayo couldn't really complain about her wildness, though:
he was the guy she cheated with, and when he met her, he himself was as
drunk as a nun full of rum. They met where I tend bar now, The Toad. I
didn't work there then. I drank there.

I wasn't there the night they met. I was taking my mother to get
chemo—but that's an entirely different story. Anyway, Mayo took Joan
home that night, got her naked, and *didn't* do it. If you got naked and didn't
do it back then, people thought you were crazy. Mayo said he didn't do it
that night because Joan was, as he said, cuter than Raquel Welch as a child.
Which, I guessed then, meant he loved her. He wanted to impress her, he
said. Though he didn't immediately: first thing the morning after, she asked
him if he'd enjoyed it. After he told her what they hadn't done, she made
him breakfast and they took a walk, and from then on, she spent every
moment she could beside him.

■　■　■

I met Joan two nights after Mayo did. I was taking classes in a nurse's aide program at the time. I'd started out in pre-med like anyone who wants money, but then, of course, came Chemistry. Then came nursing, then a nurse's aide program. What I finally did pass was bartending school.

I was drinking JD at The Toad when Joan and I met. Mayo was out of town fishing with Perney, one of those guys who—back then—I knew but just didn't like. Half an hour before last call, the lights went on, and two middle-aged men and a young woman were crawling around under some tables. Someone lose something? I said, and the woman glanced at me. She was cute in a wholesome way, the type of cute Mayo liked—I should have guessed she was the one he'd taken home two nights earlier. Her eyes sort of squinted in that sexy kind of way, and she pointed at me and yelled, Buddha!

Buddha? I said.

Yeah! she said. That god they have there in Japan!

She's been drinking, Pal, one of the middle-aged men said.

And I lost my contact, she said. She reached between the tables toward a straight Scotch, dipped in her finger and put her finger in her mouth.

Don't get fresh with her, one of the guys told me. She doesn't really know what she's doing.

She reached for his hair. It looked like a toupee. Teejay's my friend, she said.

Don't, he said.

I don't need to, she said. Because I found the American Buddha! She climbed onto a chair and hugged me. My gut, when her arms squeezed my thighs, pressed against her head: for the first time in my life, I felt fat.

I've been drinking too much, I told her.

That's what gives you the Buddha belly! she said.

How you getting home, Joan? Teejay asked her.

Buddha, she said.

Teejay glared at me. I may be fat but that's definitely a toupee, I told myself, and I smiled at him, my way of saying *Go ahead and take the first punch.*

We need to find, Joan said.

Find what? I said.

My contact.

I got on my hands and knees and ran my hands over the floor. I felt dust and sticky, dry beer. I don't think it's down here, I said, and Joan sat on a chair beside me. Under her makeup were freckles. Her eyelashes were long and black from mascara, and, hanging from one, something glistened. I stood on my knees and reached for it.

Contact? she said.

Contact, I said.

■　■　■

As Joan and I walked from my Skylark to her apartment, I had to grab her to keep her from falling. At her door, she fished around in her fake Gucci purse as if her keychain were the size of a crumb. As soon as you're in, I told her, I'll leave.

You'll leave, she mumbled. When I say. She seemed to be trying to push her fist through the bottom of her purse. There, she said. She tried three keys before she found the right one. She opened the door, and I flipped on a light, and we stood looking at an unmade bed in a cheap studio.

Home, she said.

Looks nice, I said.

You wanna feel how nice? she asked.

I helped her over the threshold and said, I think I should go.

No, you don't, she said. Because I want to be tucked in by Buddha.

■　■　■

Mayo returned from fishing a night before he was supposed to. At The Toad for our usual pitcher, he began talking about how unbelievably the white bass were biting.

Then why'd you come back early? I asked between sips.

To see someone, he said.

That woman you met? I said.

She and I prefer the term girl, he said. As in. He raised his eyebrows. Little.

I stretched a sip into a swig, hoping we hadn't slept with the same woman. Another cute one, huh? I asked, looking away.

Yeah, he said. I can't stay away from that type.

I'm glad I don't have that problem, I said, and after I swallowed my next swig, I felt fatter than I had when Joan met me.

■　■　■

Mayo and Joan dated for four years after I slept with her. We all became pals, she and I usually acting as if I were her older brother. I doubt she told Mayo what she and I did, because people who drink usually don't mention those things. Sometimes I'd forget she and I'd done it, and sometimes I'd think it didn't matter because we'd been drunk, and often it wouldn't bother me. Before she quit drinking, which Mayo insisted she do before they got engaged, she'd flirt with me, but only when she was loaded, and always in front of Mayo, and usually in a way that made Mayo act like he liked her more.

After she quit drinking, she never flirted. She and Mayo rarely came to The Toad then, and Joan began behaving like a saint, which I don't think Mayo could handle. I mean obviously he didn't want her boozing and sleazing around, but a guy that age who drinks himself doesn't know what to do with a woman who suddenly doesn't—see, his choices for entertainment seem all at once gone.

After she quit, guys at The Toad, especially Perney, told stories about her, stories I never told Mayo, and the night before she quit I saw her at The Toad with this overweight bleached-blond nursing student—I think her name was Kate—who used Joan's looks to meet men in bars. When Mayo and I stopped in for a shot that night, Joan was more out of it than she'd been when she'd slept with me, and she was getting the usual attention drunk women get from men in bars, and, at first, she and Mayo ignored each other. Then she waved him over, and they talked. Then they began arguing, and Mayo left the bar yelling and flailing his arms, probably, now that I look back on it, his way of telling himself that booze was getting the best of him. At last call, Joan and Kate were playing bar dice with two businessmen with wedding ring tan lines, and I thought about offering Joan a ride home, but I was so drunk I didn't trust myself, so I left by myself, and the next day Mayo told me Joan quit. I suspected she did with one of those businessmen what Mayo possibly feared she did with me. What I didn't know then—and what Mayo and Joan probably didn't suspect—was that you should never quit drinking for someone else. Because when you do that, whoever you quit for becomes your booze, your thing you just have to have, and later, when that someone isn't around, you are in serious, serious trouble.

■   ■   ■

I quit drinking for The Ibis two years ago. This was ten years after Mayo and Joan moved to New York, two years after they divorced, maybe six months after Joan returned to Omaha and again began visiting The Toad—first, as a bored sober person, and then, more and more, as a drinker. I don't know exactly why she and Mayo divorced, but I've had my ideas, and now that I've tended bar this long, my ideas are about confirmed. I mean you hear a lot of stories tending bar, the most common The Drinker's Divorce Story, and The Drinker's Divorce Story goes like this: two people meet in a bar, drink, and go home together; two people date, get engaged, and get married; one person quits drinking, the other keeps drinking, and the two people hate each other's guts. Everyone who tells me this story gets sad when they tell it, but then I serve them their order and they walk off toward the crowd, and, minutes later, I see them laughing. Sometimes, while absorbing the laughter, I tell myself that at age thirty-eight I've been tending bar longer than anyone should. I tell myself I should quit, or at least quit drinking, which brings me back to the saga of me and The Ibis.

■   ■   ■

The Ibis and I have been lovers, but only when we've been drunk, and during our mornings after, The Ibis has been silent as concrete. During the afternoons following these mornings, she's hung around my apartment, eating and napping and joking with me as if she's my wife, and then she'll begin picking up my things, my albums and clothes and what-not, and I'll tell her to stop, but she won't. The last time she kept picking up things, in fact the last time she stayed over, she told me she could never marry me—as if I'd proposed—then whined about how she couldn't marry me because my apartment was what she sees in me personally. *A mess too full of beer,* is how she put it. I didn't answer, just began picking up the empty bottles I could find on the floor, and then she said I wasn't understanding what she was trying to tell me. It took her awhile to tell me this; first she said *physically unattractive,* but then she went on about her other lovers, about how they'd all been athletes and so forth, about how sleek and hard their bodies were, and then, after I threw a bottle at the wall so hard it shattered, we both knew I understood. Don't clean your apartment, she was saying. Clean up your act and lose weight. Six months later I quit drinking to lose weight, only I did it for her and not for me, and then she began refusing to see me at all, and I was in trouble.

■　■　■

The Ibis is skinny, but she calls herself The Ibis for an additional reason: she's too tall to find herself a husband. See, all that talk about men liking tall women flies out the window when the woman is taller than the man. A guy might sleep with a woman taller than him, maybe even date her, but ninety-nine times out of 100 he won't marry her. He won't marry her—like The Ibis won't marry me—because that's just the way men are. It's a mean distinction for men to make, yes, but that's beside my point. My point is why I still love The Ibis despite the fact that I no longer like her: because I know that whenever she and I have lain talking on my pull-out couch in the dark, we've agreed that we're essentially the same person.

■ ■ ■

About a year after I quit drinking for The Ibis—and roughly a year and a half after Joan returned from New York—Joan walked into The Toad. It was a Saturday afternoon, and she was skinny and smiling and looking like a saint all over again, as if she'd never divorced Mayo or slept with me or anyone.

What's the smile about? I asked her.

Sobriety, she said. I'm seeing how it feels the second time around.

And?

It's just as boring, she said. But I'm happy.

I didn't like hearing she was bored, then realized why I didn't: because I, on the wagon for The Ibis despite the fact that The Ibis was ignoring me, was facing boredom myself. And then—as if maturing thirty-eight years in one moment—I realized that inhibition can be a person's most attractive feature, and I wanted to flick the towel off my shoulder and grab Joan's hand and walk us both the hell out of there. I wanted to do something sober but uninhibited, like running through a cub scout picnic in a park, with all the picnickers, especially the drinking parents, watching us as if we were crazy, me overweight and sweating, Joan lagging behind me and picturing the muscled way I felt when I slept with her all those years ago—on that night we didn't know we both knew Mayo. I wanted to run through that picnic twice, then kiss Joan on the forehead and go home and sleep alone, then run with Joan the following day and every day until the day I died. I wanted to clean my apartment whenever I came home from running, and keep running despite the fact that I was slim, and, one day, while running, bump into The Ibis.

Joan pointed at my gut and said, Looks like Buddha's gotten a smidge bigger.

I considered saying something to hurt her back, maybe hinting at the worst story Perney told about her after she'd quit booze the first time. Yes, I said. He has.

Sorry, she said. I didn't mean to hurt your feelings.

Bartenders don't have feelings, I said. I suppose you want a Diet Coke?

She nodded and I opened her a can. I set it down and filled a glass with ice, and she took them and walked to a table. She sat alone, facing away from me, and I wondered if she were waiting for someone.

She drank four Diet Cokes by herself, which, of course, attracted the drunkest of men there to her. She talked to each of them, smiling at some, and, one by one, they bought her mixed drinks.

At six-thirty, eight full cocktail glasses sat on her table. Then Teejay, the same guy who'd been with her the first night I met her, walked in. Teejay was a regular so I knew him enough to say hi, but I never did like him—because he seduced college girls with tequila.

When he sat beside Joan, I shuddered: I just wanted Joan to stay sober. He left her to start a tab with two Johnny Walkers, then took them to her table and sat facing her. She pushed her Johnny Walker toward him; she pointed to it as they talked; she lifted it, studied it, and sipped. Booze beats boredom, I thought, and I licked the Johnny Walker I'd spilled off the side of my finger, then splashed half a shot into a glass. Then we were all drinking—me, Joan, Teejay, and everyone there—and I told myself that alcohol wasn't so bad. Teejay ordered two doubles, and Joan winked at me, and I hated our weakness so much I began sweating. Four people walked in and ordered four beers, and this couple, two people married to people who weren't there, began laughing about a Drinker's Divorce Story. Teejay bought two shots of Jack, and then Joan was sloshed: I could tell by how shrill her laugh was.

Three hours later, she and Teejay left. An hour after that, she came back. She walked to the jukebox and stood facing it and kept wiping her eyes with her palm.

I locked the register and walked over. Everything okay? I asked.

Oh, everything's wonderful, she said. Her hair was matted in the back and she was pushing jukebox buttons even though the jukebox wasn't plugged in. My regulars were staring at her—or maybe at me—and then four guys walked in, including Perney, the guy Mayo went fishing with the weekend Joan and I met.

Diet Coke on the house? I asked her.

No, she said. She kept pushing those buttons. Please just leave me alone.

I returned to the bar, where Perney and his friends ordered two pitchers. Perney's friends sat down and Perney walked over to the jukebox, and he and Joan began talking. My sweating grew warmer, and Joan left The Toad, and Perney stepped back to his table and sipped beer. Then he walked up to the bar.

Need a time-out from your buds? I asked him.

No, he said. Not yet, anyway. He sat down and, staring at the mirror on the wall behind me, shook his head.

What's wrong? I asked.

That Teejay guy, he said.

What about him?

I guess he roughed up Joan pretty good.

I know he got her drunk, I said.

He took her home with him, Perney said. And wouldn't take no for an answer.

I didn't know what to say—whether I should sound angry, drunk or sad—and Perney didn't say anything either, just faced the mirror and grimaced.

Should we pay the man a visit? I asked.

I was sure Perney would grin. He kept staring at the mirror, and—just to get him talking—I poured him a bourbon on the house. He chugged it and said, A visit might work. Let's try one as soon as you're done closing.

He sat on that stool for an hour, his buddies ribbing him from their table, neither he nor I speaking as I served the laughing couple a few shots. Then he slid off the stool and left.

Five minutes before closing, he returned. He nursed a beer as I cleared out the regulars and picked his fingernails while I counted the night's gross. When The Toad had that clean calm it has only after the register is empty, I walked to the door, about to key off the lights, and said, Ready?

He followed me out the door sort of mechanically—as if he and I were finishing a first date. We can take my car, he said.

I locked up and followed him across the street to a '78 Dodge. Two softball bats, one aluminum and one wooden, lay on the floor in front of the front passenger seat. Halfway to West Omaha, I asked, How do you know where?

She told me, he said.

We didn't speak again until he turned off the ignition. Then he said, It's two blocks down. A yellow house with a black and white mailbox.

He got out of the car and took the aluminum bat and slid it up the sleeve of his jacket. I did the same with the wooden bat, and, side by side, we walked the two blocks.

The windows of the yellow house were dark. He's probably passed out, Perney said. We cut across the front yard as if crashing an after-hours party, then headed around the house to the back door. When I was set to ring the bell, Perney grabbed my forearm. No need, he said, and he stepped back and lashed out a kick that opened the door, bounced it off a wall inside, and closed it again. He kicked again, softly, and walked in. We pulled the bats from our sleeves and I found a switch on the wall; a light went on and we walked through a kitchen and an L-shaped hallway. Pictures of people, family, I guessed, lined the hallway, and at the top of the staircase was a short hall and two closed doors. As Perney opened the door to our right, I wondered if Teejay owned a gun. Perney walked into the dark room and, matter-of-factly, as if about to kiss a child goodnight, said, Say your prayers, fucker, because it's about to happen.

A light went on. A fish tank with big yellow and red fish sat on a dresser near a king-sized bed. On the bed was a clump of sheets, and under the sheets was a body. Perney yanked off the sheets and Teejay lifted his head. Naked, he was surprisingly slim, and his toupee was off, and the sour way he squinted made me hate him more than I had in The Toad.

We heard you had a date tonight, Perney said. And that your date didn't exactly have fun.

Cut the crap, Perney, Teejay said, and Perney swung. I pictured Joan laughing that shrill laugh, and I felt myself swing, my first thud not as loud as I'd expected. My third thud made a cracking sound—wood or shin bone or both—and then I wasn't the drunk me or the sober me or the young me or the old me: I was everyone's madman, everyone's lover, everyone's hater, everyone's drunk. I was a lonely spouse, a parentless child, an out-of-breath runner; I was Mayo and Joan and The Ibis and me whenever we heard The Drinker's Divorce Story. Perney's bat hit the face before mine did, and for awhile my thuds sounded louder than his, but then the sweet spot of my bat hit the nose. Then we took turns hitting the skull, grunting and swinging until the eyes opened.

We left the sheets on the floor and the bedroom light on. We said nothing as Perney drove to The Toad. When I stepped out of his car, he said, Later.

I drove my Skylark back to my apartment with my radio off. As I pulled into my parking spot, the wooden bat sat on my passenger seat just as Mayo used to in the days when he and I drank together—just as Joan did on that night I believed I was simply a man doing a young woman a favor. I thought about hiding the bat in my trunk or driving to the landfill and heaving it in, then asked myself, What for?

Inside my apartment, I closed the door behind me and let the bat lean upside-down against the wall. I walked among the things covering my floor; The Ibis once called them junk, but, to me, now that I was drinking again, they were my things. I walked past part of my inheritance—my mother's old china, lying in need of washing under crumpled napkins and the plastic spoons and forks I get whenever I visit a drive-thru. I walked past old albums I should have listened to more often, as well as the turntable I bought from Mayo before he moved to New York, and mail I got from people but never answered, and my phone and my answering machine and crumpled cans. Most of the cans were Bud sixteen-ouncers, but there were Diet Coke cans there, too, and there was an old Slurpee cup with two of those red straws that kids use as spoons, and the shorts I wore on the first warm day last spring, and The Ibis's baby oil from the afternoon she and I sunbathed before the last night we made love. Two bottles stood on either side of the baby oil, the beer The Ibis finished just after we sunbathed and the one I only began, and bottles, I admit, stood on one side or another of just about everything, but none of them had ever contained hard liquor, and most of the Bud bottles were Bud Lites. And some of the bottles were open but completely full, from the nights I used to fall asleep while talking to The Ibis's answering machine, and, as I noticed the bottles, I knew there were more of them than any one person should have in any one room, but sandwich wrappers lay everywhere, too, and I walked among the wrappers and the bottles telling myself that I should eat less and quit drinking, and I sat on my pull-out couch. I sat with the back of my head against the wall and rubbed the palm of my right hand, feeling that soreness you feel from the sting of a bat cracking, and, after my eyes closed themselves about halfway—about as much as they wanted—I sighed and thought: These are your things.

About the Author

*T*he *Los Angeles Times* said Mark Wisniewski's novel *Confessions of a Polish Used Car Salesman* "maintains what V. S. Pritchett called the 'grinning horror' of *Huckleberry Finn.*" Over 100 of Mark's stories and poems have been published in magazines including *The Virginia Quarterly Review, The Yale Review, The Missouri Review, Paris Transcontinental, Indiana Review, Paris/Atlantic, Mississippi Review, Fiction International, Prism International, The Sun, New Letters, ONTHEBUS, River Styx,* and *Poetry.* He is the recipient of a Pushcart Prize and a two-year Regents' Fellowship in Creative Writing from the University of California, Davis, where he studied under Clarence Major, Elizabeth Tallent, and Max Byrd.

Formerly the Fiction Editor of the *California Quarterly* and *New York Stories,* he has led fiction workshops in California, Texas, Pennsylvania, and New York City; he currently teaches fiction writing for the UC Berkeley Extension.

Despite a JD from Georgetown University, he has, thus far, avoided the practice of law. *All Weekend with the Lights On* is his first collection of short stories.

PRAISE FOR MARK WISNIEWSKI'S PREVIOUS WORK

"Confessions of a Polish Used Car Salesman maintains what V. S. Pritchett called the 'grinning horror' of *Huckleberry Finn."*

—Michael Harris in the *Los Angeles Times*

"A spectacular talent."

—C. Michael Curtis, Senior Editor, *The Atlantic Monthly*

"No writer I know can make dialog crackle and pop like Mark Wisniewski."

—Clarence Major, author of *Dirty Bird Blues*

"Wisniewski is one of a kind—a bright new talent in the sales lot of American fiction."

—Jay Neugeboren, author of *Imagining Robert*

"Mark Wisniewski rips the guts from his youth on the south side of Milwaukee. An excellent par none journeyman word mechanic, he puts it all together in a Hemingwayesque tale with a double shot of Bukowski. *Confessions of a Polish Used Car Salesman* is an adventure into Polish-American life. Wisniewski has a style and voice that draw the reader into his world. A kid growing up poor, with observations beyond his years. Every locale, genuine Brewski city. Sinister characters. Flim-flam car tricksters. Love. Vintage autos. All spun into a vortex metaphor of fantasma. A read that will stick to your ribs and heart, long after the last page is turned, long after the last bite of kielbasa is washed down with an icy Pabst Blue Ribbon.

— Catfish McDaris, author of *Bitchslapped*